THE BEAR NOBODY WANTED

THE BEAR
NOBODY WANTED

Janet and Allan Ahlberg

VIKING

VIKING

Published by the Penguin Group
Penguin Books Ltd, 27 Wrights Lane, London w8 5tz, England
Penguin Books USA Inc., 375 Hudson Street, New York, New York 10014, USA
Penguin Books Australia Ltd, Ringwood, Victoria, Australia
Penguin Books Canada Ltd, 10 Alcorn Avenue, Toronto, Ontario, Canada m4v 3b2
Penguin Books (NZ) Ltd, 182–190 Wairau Road, Auckland 10, New Zealand

Penguin Books Ltd, Registered Offices: Harmondsworth, Middlesex, England

First published 1992
1 3 5 7 9 10 8 6 4 2

Text and illustrations copyright © Janet and Allan Ahlberg, 1992

The moral right of the author and illustrator has been asserted

Consultant Designer: Douglas Martin
Filmset in Monophoto 14/16½ pt Bembo, by Clays Ltd, St Ives plc
Printed in Great Britain by William Clowes Limited, Beccles and London

A CIP catalogue record for this book is available from the British Library

ISBN 0–670–83982–5

ACKNOWLEDGEMENTS

The authors and publishers gratefully acknowledge the kind permission
of the copyright holders to include extracts from the following songs
in this book:

'Stormy Weather' (Harold Arlen/Ted Koehler) © 1933, Mills Music
Inc., USA/EMI United Partnership Ltd, used by permission; 'My Blue
Heaven' (George Whiting/Walter Donaldson) © 1927, EMI United
Partnership Ltd/Memory Lane Music, used by permission; 'Look for
the Silver Lining' (Buddy De Sylva/Jerome Kern) used by kind
permission of Redwood Music Ltd, Iron Bridge House, 3 Bridge
Approach, London NW1 8BD and © Polygram International
Publishing/Warner Chappell Music, reproduced by permission; 'You
Are My Sunshine' (Davis/Mitchell) used by kind permission of
Southern Music Publishing Company Ltd, 8 Denmark Street, London
WC2H 8LT.

Contents

[1]

How a Bear Was Made

THIS IS HOW a bear was made many years ago. The materials used were: brown plush for the fur, velvet or felt for the paws, and strong black thread for the nose and mouth. In addition the following things were needed: one pair of glass eyes, five disc joints for attaching the head, arms and legs to the body, and lots of kapok or wood wool for the filling. Sometimes an extra item such as a squeaker was included. Ribbons, too, usually red and in the form of a bow, were popular then. Last but not least by any means, there was the label with the maker's name. This was printed on a silky material, just perfect, as we all know or can remember, for stroking between the fingers at bedtime and sending ourselves off to sleep.

Now the particular bear this story is about was made in a teddy-bear factory. Here at a long table a number of women or young girls would sit. (You could start work at fourteen in those days.) Each would make one part of a bear, or concentrate on the sewing, filling or whatever, then pass it on to the next. In this way the materials – plush and kapok, velvet and thread – moved down the table slowly taking on the shape and appearance of a bear. The bears, as it were, *materialized* from the piles of stuff and the busy fingers of the women.

Every stage in the process was important, but one stage was vital. This was the stitching of the nose and mouth, and the positioning of the eyes. The women who did this job were called 'finishers', and theirs was the most skilled work of all. Just one slip with the needle or mistake in the positioning of the eyes could change a bear's expression from cheerful to grumpy, trustworthy to sly, and ruin his life forever. For how a bear looked, especially when he was new, was how he *was*. His character was formed from the outside. It isn't fair, I know. It was hardly a bear's fault if things went wrong. But that is how it was.

Well, as you will see, the particular bear this story is about was to suffer in just this way. For as soon as his eyes were in his head, and his nose and mouth were stitched below them, this little bear was filled with a sense of his own importance (as filled as he was with kapok). All of us have this feeling, of course, to some extent; but with this bear the conviction was too strong. It made him instantly proud and selfish. A couple of misplaced stitches, that's all it took; a bit of crookedness about the eyes, and the job was done.

AS EACH BEAR completed his journey down the table, he was put on a trolley with the others. Here he had a grandstand view of more bears being made, and could begin to puzzle out his surroundings (and his own existence!).

It was a curious business with new-made bears. Only a little while ago they had been piles of fabric, spools of thread, sacks of kapok. And yet now here they were, *knowing* things. I suppose it was a sort of instinct, really. The way a baby bird, for instance, will crouch when it sees the shadow of a hawk. Whatever it was, these new-made bears knew things from the start; not just that they were 'bears' or 'made', but other things, too. Words like 'shop' and 'present' already had some meaning for them; words like 'child' as well, and 'bedtime' and 'belonging'.

But this particular bear, from the moment *he* was made, had thoughts only of himself. Why, almost the first thing that he ever saw, while still on the table, was himself. One of the women had a tin box – full of eyes, as it happened. The box was open, and the bear was able to see his reflection in its shiny surface. It was a sight that captivated him at once, and – so it seemed – for ever. 'Oh, what a bear!' he thought. Later, as he sat on the trolley with the others, he felt an urge to flinch from contact with them. There were all kinds of bears on that trolley: big and little, expensive and cheap, with ribbons and without. There were brown bears, yellow bears, even white bears. There were bears in sailor suits and baby bears with bibs. Oh, yes, such a variety! And yet our bear felt superior to them all. He even felt superior to bears who were more or less identical to him. He found things wrong with every one of them (those he could see, anyway): the shape of an ear, perhaps, or the stitching of a velvet paw.

When the trolley was full, it was wheeled to another part of the factory and an empty one put in its place. This journey was always a great adventure for the brand-new bears. They saw fresh sights at every turn: a fire-extinguisher – a clock – a man! They passed through pools of light and areas of shade. From the motion of the trolley, they felt the breeze for the first time on their fur. As they were taken down a corridor, the new bears heard the clanking of typewriters, the ringing of phones. At the front entrance they caught a glimpse – on a table, on a blue silk cloth – of a small display of bears. Most were splendid creatures, fine examples of the factory's range. But one, surprisingly, was old and worn. His ribbon had become a tattered, faded string; his body itself, in many places, gone quite bald.

The trolley continued on its way and was eventually left in a far corner of the factory side by side with other trolleys. Time passed. At half-past five the factory workers went home and the cleaners arrived. At half-past seven the cleaners left and the nightwatchman took over. Meanwhile, in their shadowy corner of the factory, the new bears on the trolleys talked. For bears can talk, in case you didn't know; though their voices are soft and difficult to hear, unless you have the ears of a bear. Children who know their bears well can sometimes hear them, but grown-ups, hardly ever.

The bears talked of their hopes and fears; what sort of shop they might be sold in; what kind of child they might eventually belong to. Our bear took no part in these conversations. He felt the other bears were beneath him (even those on the shelf above); also, he had already decided who *he'd* belong to. 'A "princess" in a "palace",' he thought; it had to be that, or possibly a young duke. For our bear, sad to say, was as much a snob about people as he was about bears. He even looked down on the women – 'factory workers' – who had made him. His own mothers, when you come to think of it.

But one part of the conversation did interest him. It had to do with that old bear they had seen on display. Some of the more timid or gloomy bears – for the others had characters, too – were most upset. They had not thought a bear could become so . . . battered.

A large bear on a neighbouring trolley offered an explanation. 'A bear told me,' he said, 'that bear is on display to demonstrate the popularity of factory-made bears.'

'Yes,' said another. 'I heard a woman from the office saying, "That is a well-loved bear."'

'"A well-loved bear",' said the first. 'Yes, I heard that.'

Whereupon the phrase was taken up and repeated

by many of the newest bears, though not our bear. He just sat picturing in his mind the threadbare bear, and promising himself to keep well clear of 'love', if that was what it did to you.

At that moment a baby bear on the bottom shelf let out a startled cry: 'Oh!' But there was nothing to fear; it was only the factory cat prowling in search of mice. (So there was something to fear, for the mice, I suppose.) A couple of the braver bears called out to the cat as it passed, 'Puss, puss!' They admired its 'living' fur, and would have stroked it, if they could. And then a torch beam split the dark, and lots of bears said, 'Sh!' It was the watchman on his rounds. He paused beside the trolleys and shone his torch from side to side. The light bounced back from scores of polished eyes. Then darkness came again, and all was silent.

[2]

The Bin

THE NEXT MORNING at half-past seven the new bears were wheeled into the Inspection and Packing Department. Standards at the bear factory were high. Every bear was thoroughly inspected and only those in perfect condition were sent to the shops. The inspector sat at a table with a trolley of bears beside him. He wore a white coat. On the table was a pair of scissors, a magnifying glass, a tape-measure and a short ruler. Standing next to the inspector was his apprentice, a boy of fifteen. At twenty-five to eight the boy took a bear from the trolley and placed it on the table. The inspection began.

Our bear sat in his place and watched the inspector

at work. Other bears watched, too; nervously or hopefully or gloomily waiting their turn. One extremely modest and pessimistic bear was even shivering. He felt sure that when it *was* his turn, he'd fail. Our bear, of course, thought the opposite. He wondered if there was a prize for the outstanding bear.

All that morning, except for a tea break, the inspector and his apprentice inspected bears. What they were looking for were flaws in the materials or shoddy workmanship. Small flaws, a bit of hanging thread, for example, or a loose eye, meant only that a bear was returned to the workshop and repaired. Larger flaws, however, such as a badly shaped head, or when the fabric was sub-standard, meant something else. Yes, large flaws meant . . . the bin.

The rejection bin – more like a basket, really – stood next to the inspector's chair. Now and then, a bear went into it. After all, the inspector had his job to do. In some ways a pile of bears in the bin at the end of the day was the only proof that he had done it. The new-made bears on the trolley could see the bin, and had heard about it, anyway. Rumours from previous generations of bears had been passed back to them. They had whispered about it in the night. Some had not slept because of it.

At two o'clock our bear was taken down and placed on the table. The inspector adjusted his spectacles. He manipulated the bear's arms and legs, examined his stitching and stared into his little face. The bear stared back. The truth is, he inspected the inspector's face. Nor did he approve of what he saw. Oh, no – this inspector, in his opinion, was not well made himself. His moustache was straggly and his eyebrows were not level; also, his spectacles could have done with a polish.

So the bear formed a low opinion of the inspector. Meanwhile, as you've probably guessed, the inspector formed a low opinion of him. He didn't care for the bear's expression. He didn't like to be looked down on by a bear. Whoever would buy a bear that looked like that?

Now changing a bear's expression at this stage was a nearly impossible business. The fur fabric had been trimmed to the shape of the existing nose and mouth, so any alterations would show. And if you moved the eyes, this would show as well, especially with a new bear. Consequently there was nothing to be done. The inspector spoke to his apprentice, the apprentice nodded, and the bear – the proudest bear in the factory – was put in the bin.

Well, this was not the worst thing that ever happened to this bear, but it was the most shocking. I mean, we may have guessed it was coming, but he had no idea at all. 'Pride goeth before destruction,' the Bible says, 'and an haughty spirit before a fall.' Still, there was a soft landing for him, at least, on the other bears already in there.

Our bear, when he realized what had happened, was outraged. How dare they throw him in the bin. Him! At the same time it crossed his mind that it was all a terrible mistake. Soon they would pull him out and apologize. It also occurred to him to protest – yell – demand a second inspection. However, upside-down with his face pushed into the furry front of another bear, there was little chance he would be heard.

But if the bin was a bad thing, after the bin was worse. You see, it was the fate of all those poor, discarded bears in the coming days to be *un-made*: to have their stitches cut, their stuffing removed and their eyes returned to the eye box. ('Ashes to ashes, dust to dust, kapok to kapok.') Later on, these various parts would be re-used – recycled – to make more bears.

Fortunately it didn't hurt a bear to be made – all that stitching, for instance, quite painless – and it didn't hurt him to be un-made. Furthermore none of the bears in the bin or on the trolleys knew what was coming. There were no rumours about *this*, for the good reason that there were no bears to spread them.

But, of course, the rejected bears – here comes another! – were far from happy. Small sobs and groans could be heard (by the bears themselves, if not the inspector) in the depths of the bin. The shame of being thrown out, the disappointment of not going to a shop, fear of the unknown, all played their part in the general misery. Nevertheless our bear, it must be said, was fairly unafraid. His pride, though dented, was still intact. If people threw him in a bin, more fools they. As the afternoon wore on, he felt a growing urge to flinch from contact with his fellow sufferers, inferiors every one.

[3]

Mrs Broom

AT THE END of the day the workers once more went home and the cleaners arrived. The acceptable bears had been packed into boxes and moved to the Despatch Department. The rejected bears still languished in the bin. They would be dealt with tomorrow. At seven o'clock the bears in the bin were roused from their troubled thoughts by the sound of singing:

'Daisy, Daisy, give me your answer, do.
I'm half crazy, all for the love of you.'

The singer was one of the cleaners, singing as she swept the floor and approached the bin. Her name, believe it or not, was Mrs Broom. (Actually, Mrs

Broom had a sister named Mrs Pye, and she worked in a cake shop.) Mrs Broom was a solid-looking woman with strong forearms and red cheeks. She had a poorly paid job and a large family. Understandably, perhaps, she was inclined now and then to take a bear from the bin and put it into her bag. Of course, the cleaners were not supposed to take things; it was called 'pilfering'. Mrs Broom had to be careful that the supervisor didn't see her. All the same, it wasn't stealing, really, she told herself. These bears were rejects anyway.

Well, that evening Mrs Broom slipped a furtive hand into the bin, grabbed a bear by the leg, hastily admired its red bow and velvet paws, failed to notice its expression, and pushed it into her bag. She continued to sing as she did all this:

'It won't be a stylish marriage,
I can't afford a carriage.'

Singing provided an innocent cover for what she was up to:

'But you'll look sweet on the seat'

and was her habit, anyway.

'Of a bicycle made for two.'

Meanwhile a bewildered bear – our bear, you realize – was struggling to make sense of what had happened. For a moment his hopes had risen. Hooray! It was the rescue he'd half-expected, with the apology he so fully deserved soon to follow. Then, from being upside-down in a bin, he found himself upside-down in a bag, and an uncomfortable one at that. There was a hard purse full of hard money digging into his head. It was a smelly bag, too; lately used for carrying brussels sprouts and old newspapers.

The bear in the bag remained bewildered. What was this woman up to, he wondered. Was it part of her job to put him in a bag? It seemed unlikely. And what was this hard thing sticking into his head – and what were these smells – and who was 'Daisy'?

At half-past seven Mrs Broom put on her hat and coat and left the factory. It was light outside – a warm May evening – but the bear was unable to see a thing. Not only was he upside-down, but Mrs Broom had covered him with a headscarf, just in case. But if he couldn't see, he could certainly hear – and what sounds! The judder and clang of a tram – a barking dog – a mower – bird-song – laughter! A sense of the hugeness of the world passed rapidly through the little bear. 'What *is* this place?' he thought. 'Where *is* she taking me?'

Then voices (and a sizzling sound).

'Evening, Mrs Broom. The usual?'

'Evening, Charlie. Yes, please.' Mrs Broom's large hand came down into the bag. She squeezed the bear aside and fumbled for her purse.

'Nice weather for the time of year.'

'Oh, lovely!'

More sizzling. A pause. The sound of whistling. Suddenly, a substantial parcel of fish and chips was levered into the bag on top of the instantly indignant bear. Then Mrs Broom said, 'Bye, Charlie!' and stepped out into the street.

WHEN MRS BROOM and her fish and chips arrived home, they received a fine welcome. Mrs Broom's eldest daughter was at the door, her second daughter took her bag, her son came running down the stairs to greet her, and her husband put the kettle on. Even the cat brushed up against her legs. Only the baby, snoozing in her cot upstairs, was missing. The table was laid and the bread and butter prepared. The plates were warming in the oven.

If the bear had been able to observe this welcome, he might have supposed it was for him (and about time, too). As it was, when Mrs Broom did remove him from her bag and he saw *children* in the room, his

hopes once more went sky high. He had, as you know, never seen a child before. Unluckily for him, these children had seen lots of bears, especially in recent weeks since their mother had started work at the factory. Thus his interest in them was not matched by theirs in him. They were not bowled over, for instance, as he quite expected them to be. No, what they cared more about was the fish and chips.

When supper was over, the bear was examined briefly by all three children, then tossed aside on the sofa. Mr Broom had a look at him and accidentally dropped cigarette ash on his head. Later, the cat jumped up and gave him a sniff. Otherwise he was ignored. The girls made a den in the clothes horse and played with their dolls. The boy tried playing with a wooden fort, but was told to get ready for bed. Mr Broom washed up and Mrs Broom dried. She sang another song, and hummed when she forgot the words:

'You are my sunshine,
Hm hm hm hm hm.
You make me happy
When skies are grey.'

Whereupon a canary, which the bear had not noticed before, chipped in (chirruped in) with its own song. It also kicked some seed from its cage onto the sofa . . . and the bear.

'You'll never know, dear,
How much I love you.
Please don't take
My sunshine away.'

Eventually it got dark outside. (So the sunshine was taken away.) The curtains were drawn and the girls went to bed. Mr and Mrs Broom listened to the radio, known in those days as the 'wireless'. They shared a jug of beer, which Mr Broom had fetched from the pub on the corner. Suddenly, the oldest girl, Marjorie, came bursting back into the room clutching a doll.

'What's all this?' said her mum.

'Won't be a minute,' said Marjorie. 'I've had an idea.'

She hurried to the sofa and picked up the bear, whose spirits again were likewise lifted. (What an optimist he was.) 'She's remembered me,' he thought. 'I'm wanted!'

Swiftly, Marjorie removed the bear's red ribbon and tied it round her doll's waist. 'Look, Mum – look, Dad – Jemima's got a sash.'

'So she has,' said her dad.

'How nice,' said her mum. 'Now – off to bed!'

That night, alone on the sofa in the darkened room, the bear considered his plight. He had lost a ribbon and gained some cigarette ash, a bit of bird seed and the still lingering smell of fish and chips. It was a poor swop. There again, at least he now 'belonged' (after a fashion) to 'children' (of a sort). What's more, he had escaped the bin.

The bear stared out across the room, lit faintly by the dying fire. A couple of other bears – also refugees from the bin – were talking softly on top of a cupboard; he could just see their feet. Some dolls were sound asleep in the clothes-horse den. The bear began to hum to himself. It was the song Mrs Broom had been singing earlier. A few of the words came back to him: 'You make me happy . . . when skies are grey'. A further consoling thought was in his mind: 'At least I am the best bear here. The best toy, come to that.' He hummed a little more, regretted again his stolen ribbon, and fell asleep.

[4]

Dolls and Washing

THE NEXT DAY – it was a Saturday – the bear's life with the Broom family really began. After breakfast, Mrs Broom complained about the clutter of toys and suchlike in the kitchen, the sitting-room, the hall – everywhere! The three older children scuttled round grabbing things and carrying them upstairs. The girls shared a room, and the boy shared one also, with the baby. It was a small house.

These were the children's names, by the way, and their ages:

Marjorie (you have met her already) – 10

Kitty – 8

George – $6\frac{1}{2}$

Louise (the baby) – 11 months.

For the first part of the morning the children had jobs to do. This was the custom in those days. Marjorie helped her mother to make the beds. Kitty ran an errand to the corner shop (the opposite corner to the pub), and took a message to her auntie, Mrs Pye. George fed the hens and collected the eggs; there was a hen-house at the end of the garden. Baby Louise, of course, had no jobs. She just sat in the yard tossing her rattle and various toys over the side of her pram – the edge of the world! – for the pure joy of seeing them disappear, and then reappear by courtesy of any member of the family who happened to be passing. Her other favourite occupation was pulling her socks off and tossing them out.

Meanwhile upstairs in a toy-box in an immensely crowded bedroom sat the bear, his eyes and ears bombarded with new sights and sounds: the zigzag pattern of the wallpaper, the rose-pink tiles around the fireplace, the brass knob on the door. There was a great clutter of books and dolls, and dolls' houses, and cardboard boxes converted into dolls' houses, and comics and Plasticine and paintboxes. The play of sunlight in the room – he had his back to the window – astounded him. It bounced about on numerous shiny surfaces: the fireplace tiles, the brass knob, pictures on the walls, the dressing-table mirror. And the sounds were no less fascinating: footsteps in the house – creaking stairs – beds being made – voices. There was the gurgle and yell of Baby Louise below the window in the yard, birds chirruping on the roof, a distant mower (again).

Yes, everything was new and marvellous, and I haven't even mentioned the smells. The bear could feel the surge of life within him, the expansion of his own small world. For a time he forgot himself in the contemplation of his surroundings. Then, eventually – inevitably – his gaze came back towards . . . the mirror.

From the angle of the mirror and his position in the toy-box, the bear was able to see only two-thirds of himself, from the shoulders down. Still, two-thirds was better than nothing. Soon the flames of his conceit were being fanned once more. How smart he looked, even without a ribbon, and how scruffy in comparison were the other toys that he could see.

At that moment Marjorie and her mother entered the room, bumped about a bit, made the bed (three-quarter size, which the girls shared), and left. Almost at once the bear's gaze returned to the mirror. Because of the bumping, its angle had shifted; now he could see himself entirely. What joy! Unfortunately, what he could also see a fair amount of was Jemima.

The bear regarded the doll's reflection. (Her actual position was on the bedside table behind him.) She was a home-made knitted doll, and roughly his size. She wore a yellow dress and had a green straw hat stitched to her head. The expression on her face, in the bear's opinion, was silly and self-satisfied. And around her waist, of course, she had his ribbon.

'That's my ribbon,' said the bear.

'*Was*,' said Jemima smugly.

'Give it back!'

'No. Besides, how can I?'

At this point, two other dolls, friends and allies of Jemima's, joined in.

'Yes, how can she?'

'Anyway, *she* didn't take it.'

'No, *Marjorie* took it.'

'And Marjorie gave it to Jemima.'

'So it's Jemima's now.'

'So there!'

The bear could feel his temper rising, particularly since part of what the dolls were saying was true. How could she give it back? She couldn't move. She could talk (more's the pity) but not walk. And it was the same for him. For some reason bears, dolls and other soft toys could see and think and talk – but they couldn't walk. Nor could they grab a stupid doll by her stupid straw hat and swing her around either. No, the truth was he couldn't chase Jemima and she couldn't run away. It was stalemate.

Well, after that the dolls made a few rude remarks about the bear's appearance:

'Look at his face!'

'Lord Muck!'

The bear resisted the urge to growl – it was un-dignified – and assumed a superior silence. In time his temper cooled. And the thought in his mind was: 'I am the best bear here, ribbon or no ribbon.'

WHEN THE CHILDREN had finished their jobs, they were allowed to play in the yard. The Brooms' house was part of a terrace: a row of houses. Behind the terrace was a shared yard where children from all the

houses played. On the far side of the yard were the
wash-houses, one per house. (In those days many
houses were without hot water. The laundry was
done in the wash-house, where water could be heated
in a boiler by means of a coal fire.) Behind the
wash-houses were narrow strips of garden, most of
which had two posts planted in them with a clothes-
line stretched between. Finally, at the far end of some
of the gardens were rabbit hutches, hen-houses,
pigeon lofts.

Marjorie and Kitty took their toys into the yard.
The more precious ones, like Jemima and her friends,
were carried separately. The rest were humped down
all higgledy-piggledy in the toy-box. George carried
his (mostly military) toys in an old enamel bucket,
and went back to get the fort.

In the yard the toy-box was placed against the wall

of the house not far from Baby Louise and her pram. Marjorie and Kitty were joined by a couple of other girls with their toys, and the 'playing' began. This involved each girl setting up a home and being the mother to a family of dolls and other toys. The girls, like gods, really, worked out the lives their toys were to lead; the triumphs they would enjoy, the disasters they would suffer. From time to time Baby Louise hurled down a thunderbolt in the shape of a rattle or a teething ring. She was a god, too. Meanwhile, from his position in the toy-box, the bear could see little. He was slumped forward facing the wall. What he had a good view of were his own feet and the brick-work. Behind him he could hear the girls' voices. From nearby came the sound of music, probably a wireless. There was a smell of smoke and fresh washing in the air. Monday was the usual wash-day, but with babies around – and Louise was not the only one – nappies were a daily chore.

Well, soon the bear was swept up into the girls' vast game. He quickly discovered that all four of them were mad about dolls, and maniacs about washing. Whatever the 'story', it seemed always to follow the same path and end in the same place. First some dolls would ride around in splendour in their pram and visit some other dolls. Both sets of dolls would be waited on and fussed over by their 'mothers'. Then a naughty 'child', usually a bear or rabbit, would throw his dinner over himself, or fall out of a 'window' into the mud (previously prepared). Finally the culprit would be told off and given a rather violent bath. Thereafter, with only minor variations, the same things would happen all over again.

Thus, during the morning and the early part of the afternoon, our bear endured his first experience of play; play being the object of a toy's existence, when you come to think of it. These were the indignities he suffered:

(1) Being dressed up in a short pink frock and a pair of baby's bootees.

(2) Being smirked at by Jemima and Co.

(3) Being pushed by Kitty out of a pram and into a muddy puddle.

(4) Being scolded by Kitty – 'You naughty girl!' – for getting his clothes dirty, and himself too.

(5) Having his clothes removed (this was no bad thing) and being soaked in cold water in an enamel bowl by Shirley, Kitty's friend, rubbed with a bar of hard green soap, and scrubbed with a nailbrush.

(6) Being abandoned on the back step to dry, while the dolls set off on another regal ride.

(7) Being smirked at by Jemima and Co.

THE BEAR sat on the step in the sunshine (and a small puddle) feeling sorry for himself. His fur was in a dreadful state, not just wet but all scuffed up. There was soap still in it and a soapy taste in his mouth. One of his ears was full of water. Beside him, slumped against each other, were a pair of miserable-looking rabbits – also wet – and a damp panda. After a while, out of the corner of his mouth, the panda spoke: 'This your first time?'

'Yes,' said the bear. He was too fed up to be stand-offish.

'You'll get used to it,' said the panda. 'The thing is, if you're not a doll in this place you've got *no* chance.'

There was a pause. One of the rabbits said, 'Yes, and if you think this lot's bad, wait till George gets you.'

'Who's George?' said the bear, forgetting for a moment the boy's name, though he had heard it earlier.

'George is . . . George,' said the other rabbit. 'You'll be begging for a bath before he's finished.'

At that moment, in his brown coat and with a basket of warm loaves on his arm, the breadman arrived. He knocked at the door, which Mrs Broom opened, causing the bear and the panda to topple over and putting an end to their conversation. When the breadman left, Mrs Broom complained about her cluttered step. Shortly afterwards she spotted some of her hair grips, which Marjorie was using on a mohair bear, and complained about that. Meanwhile our bear was propped up by himself against the wall to continue drying. There he stayed for the remainder of the day, puzzled still by the whole business of children and playing, regretting his bedraggled state, mourning his lost ribbon . . . and worrying about George.

[5]

Bad Days for a Bear . . .

IT TOOK a couple of days for the bear to dry out completely. His lower half where he had sat in the bowl was soaked right through to the kapok. Mrs Broom wouldn't allow wet toys back into the house; consequently the bear and a few others were banished to the draining-board in the wash-house. The bear's legs had lost some of their shape while having the water squeezed out of them by Kitty. If anything, his fur was even more scuffed up.

Nevertheless, as always, things could have been worse. One poor toy, a rag rabbit, had been put through the mangle, a contraption used in those days (before spin-dryers) to wring the washing out. He was in a terrible shape; well, flat, really.

During this time the bear continued to worry about George. Once or twice he heard him whistling in the yard. But the rabbits (who had warned him) together with the panda, belonged to Shirley, and so, presumably, were slumped together in her wash-house. The toys he *was* with had nothing to tell him. Either they were too sodden to speak, or didn't know anything, or were put off by his superior expression. The bear also gave thought to Jemima. He regarded her as a thief. Maybe it wasn't all her fault — or her fault at all — but she could at least have regretted what had happened and told those silly friends of hers to shut up.

Despite his worries and exasperations, however, the bear continued to find the world a fascinating place, even within the confines of a gloomy wash-house. Through a small unwashed window he could see a patch of sky. The day before, when toppling over on the step, he'd seen a great expanse of it, like a huge blue bowl above his head. And he'd marvelled then, as he marvelled now, at the vastness and variety of the world. That heavenly sight, by the way, went hand in hand with a heavenly smell: the warm loaves in the breadman's basket. It was altogether a memorable experience for the bear.

The days went by. The bear dried out and was returned to the toy-box where, sad to say, his situation did not improve. Almost at once he was set upon (his words) by Marjorie with a pair of scissors. These girls were scissor-mad, too. She snipped a disturbing amount of fur from his front and put it on a little bakelite plate

to represent some food or other in a dolls' picnic. Later
that day, at the same picnic, Baby Louise got a hold of
him with her iron grip. She was sitting on the grass in
Shirley's garden attempting to eat a toffee apple. (Marjorie and Kitty often employed Louise as a sort of
extra doll.) Well, what Louise did in the next ten
minutes was chew the bear's ear – she was teething –
dribble on his head and generally crush him with her
sticky fingers. Some of his fur ended up on the toffee
apple.

After Louise, and unnoticed by anybody except the
bear, came a puppy. This puppy sniffed him, licked
him and, before departing, widdled on him. Fortunately the puppy's aim was poor. Even so the bear's feet
smelt unpleasantly for days. He suffered much from
the embarrassment of it all, plus a further period of
detention in the wash-house. In these circumstances,
thoughts of George had faded from the bear's mind.
Consequently it came as a complete surprise one morning – a Saturday again – when George did get him.

IT HAPPENED like this: George sauntered up, hands in
pockets, whistling. He approached the toy-box, looked
left and right, grabbed the bear and stuffed him up his
jumper. Then, still whistling, he sauntered off. This
way of acquiring things to a musical accompaniment
was, of course, his mother's method. It must have run
in the family.

George took the bear to a private place he had
between the back of Mr Phipps's pigeon loft and the
rear wall of the gardens. Here, alone, or with his best

33

friend Denis Spooner, George enjoyed his supposedly secret passion: he lit fires. Actually, everybody knew that George lit fires. He was a bad boy. He sneaked matches out of the house, and wood and paper from the wash-house. When he got caught, he said he was sorry and promised never to do it again. Then, after a while . . . he did it again. But although he was bad, he wasn't deliberately cruel. George was a scientist, really. His fires were always part of an experiment. The question that fascinated him was: what happened to something when it burned?

Well, what happened to his lead soldiers was, they melted. A rubber in the shape of Mickey Mouse produced a terrible smell. The paintwork on a model racing car blistered. A tiny celluloid frog disappeared completely in a puff of smoke.

And what happened to the bear? First of all it was a horrible shock being kidnapped in that fashion and pushed up George's jumper. He knew it was George; he recognized the whistling. Also, there was the fear of the unknown: what could be worse than scissors and a mangle? Eventually, laid out on a house brick beside a little crackling fire, he got his answer.

George applied a smouldering stick to the bear's label and singed it. He did the same to one of his ears and singed that. It didn't hurt, of course, but it was frightening. The poor bear resembled a sacrifice (to the gods again), laid out on his brick. The worrying smell of singed fur hung in the air. At that moment Denis Spooner appeared with a potato that he had 'borrowed' from his grandma. For a while the bear was forgotten.

Quickly, too quickly, Denis and George cooked the
potato, or rather charred it on the outside leaving it
more or less raw in the middle. Then, with genuine
enjoyment, they ate it.

After that, alerted perhaps by the baked potato (or
burnt bear) smell, Mrs Broom arrived. Knowing what
to expect, she had half a bucket of water already with
her, which she threw on the fire. Then she smacked
George, scolded Denis and led them away. George,
despite his tears, had the grace to bring the bear along
and return him to the toy-box.

So in a way the bear got off lightly; scared, singed
but not incinerated. As he sat in the toy-box, his sense
of relief was huge. The unknown terror of George had
been confronted and survived. His label had a burnt
edge, but otherwise the singeing, brown on brown,
hardly showed. The normal sounds of Louise in her
pram, the girls skipping, a wireless, the milkman's clink-
ing bottles, soothed his nerves. His spirits once more
began to rise. Perhaps now, after all these disasters,
something good would happen.

[6]

. . . And Jemima, Too

IN THE DAYS and weeks that followed, nothing
good happened to the bear, unless you count
something bad happening to Jemima. His condition continued to deteriorate. He was worried about
the uneven shape of his legs where Kitty had wrung
him out. There was a disturbing thread hanging from
one of his paws. What's more, the rich brown velvet
of his paws was fading in the sunlight to which he was
often exposed. His expression, however, which could
have done with a change, was unaltered. He remained
a bear of great importance to himself and little
importance to others.

ONE EVENING Mrs Broom came home with fish and chips as usual, and a bear. She removed her hat and coat, handed the fish and chips to Mr Broom and tossed the bear on the sofa.

'There you are,' she said to the children; 'make the most of it. That's the last.'

Mrs Broom, you see, had finally been caught by the supervisor with a bear in her bag. She had been allowed to keep the bear, a particularly poor specimen, but had been warned about her future conduct. Mrs Broom (just like George) promised never to do it again.

The new bear was a cheaper variety than the others. He had felt, not velvet, paws and no ribbon. The number of things wrong with him was remarkable. Both his fur and stitching were sub-standard. Worse still, his head was misshapen, giving him a nervous expression and – as you now know – a character to match. Finally, and most amazingly, his legs were different lengths. However could such a bear have been made in the first place?

In our bear's eyes this new bear was – you guessed it – inferior. (There again he would have been inferior, no matter what his condition.) That night, as they sat together in the toy-box, our bear gave short, unhelpful answers to the new bear's nervous questions. He even took the opportunity to make him more nervous. 'The girls are bad enough,' he said, 'but wait till George gets you.'

The strange thing was though, a day or two later when George did get him, he liked him. Soon, in spite of his lopsided head and haunted look, or perhaps because of them, this bear became George's favourite toy. He carried him everywhere, allowed him to take part in his 'battles' (and win), and never once set fire to him.

Coincidentally, at this time another bear went up in the world. It was the mohair bear I mentioned earlier, the one who had the hair grips put in. Well, first of all tragedy struck this little bear. Shirley, with Marjorie an interested observer, tried out her dad's hair clippers on him. The results were quick and terrible. As his fur fell to the ground, the bear appeared to shrink. He ended up three-quarters bald, and an odd sight altogether. As Jemima said, 'Mohair – no hair!'

But once more the unexpected occurred. Marjorie took pity on this ridiculous bear; understandably, really, for she was partly to blame. Anyway, she found a jumper to fit him, and a tiny pair of sailor's trousers. She gave him a name – Mickey Mo – and by and by promoted him to *her* favourite toy.

Jemima and her friends watched this development with jealousy growing in their hearts. They made many spiteful comments, which did them no good at all. Our bear also witnessed what was happening, in his case with mixed feelings. He disliked Jemima and took pleasure in her downfall. But while disapproving of her jealousy (and unkindness), he failed to notice his own. *He* was jealous of *both* bears. How could anybody prefer them to him? It was a mystery, and more than that, a dreadful disappointment, and more than *that*, insulting.

The days went by and the popularity of bears continued to grow. Shirley had one for her birthday. The popularity of pandas and rabbits also grew. Eventually there was a bears' picnic with real pop and Farley's rusks, courtesy of Baby Louise. Although the girls did all the eating and drinking, the bears – rabbits and pandas, too – occupied places of honour and were at least offered food. The extremely disgruntled dolls merely sat along the wall of the washhouse, watching. To cap it all, at the end of the picnic one of them, a close friend of Jemima's, was bathed.

But if bears in a general way were popular, our bear in his particular way was not. He did attend the picnic but none of the girls fussed over him or even noticed him most of the time. And with every day that passed his situation worsened. Presently, when the toys were taken from the toy-box, our bear was left behind. Hours later, when they returned full of the excitement of the day, they were piled in on top of him. He was depressed in more ways than one.

Yet even then the candle of his conceit still flickered. If he was neglected, if inferior toys were preferred to him, so what? It simply showed what dreadful judges these children were. They wouldn't recognize a superior bear if he leapt out of a window at them.

It was now late July and the school holidays were about to begin. The Broom family had booked a week at the seaside. Certain toys, it was rumoured, might be allowed to go, if they could fit into the children's luggage, which the children themselves would carry.

Our bear, hearing the conversations the other toys were having, adopted a disdainful manner. He realized his chances of a holiday were nil. Actually, many of the toys, him included, had no idea what a holiday was, but it sounded fun. Our bear, however, pretended to dislike the whole idea. He hoped no child would put *him* in a suitcase. Oh no, he'd rather stay here in peace and quiet. As it turned out, he got peace and quiet all right – more than he bargained for.

In the week before the holiday, Mrs Broom organized her children to tidy up their possessions: clothes, school things, but most of all, toys. She also organized her husband. His hobby was woodwork. He was encouraged to sort out his piles of wood, blueprints, woodwork magazines and so on. This was a hard task for Mr Broom. 'Sorting out' really meant throwing away, and he liked to keep things. 'Might come in handy' was his favourite phrase. The children, it seemed, took after their father. They liked to keep things too. But with three children, and a baby (and a husband), in a little house, if things weren't tidied up now and then and *some* of them thrown away, the place would simply fill up like a bath and overflow. That's what Mrs Broom said. More persuasively, she pointed out that unless old things were disposed of, there'd be no room for new. And with birthdays coming up . . .

The children took the hint. They sorted out their toy-box, toy-bucket and toy-drawers. They searched behind the sofa and under the beds. They gathered a large pile of old comics, coloured-in colouring books, used-up paintboxes, pencil stubs, fragments of wax crayon and sweet papers, and a small pile of unwanted toys. The rubbish, of course, went straight into the dustbin. But the unwanted toys, for a while at least, were relegated to the wash-house. (Mr Broom had cleared it out and made a space for them.) They included the mangled rabbit (remember him?), a couple of incomplete jigsaws, a trodden-on tin whistle, a cracked yo-yo, three alphabet blocks and one partly chewed, slightly singed, deeply insulted . . . bear.

The Wash-House

THE BEAR sat on a shelf in the wash-house. For a while he tried to keep up the pretence that he was enjoying his solitude, but it was no use. For a bear as proud as he was, his situation was dreadful: unwanted by the factory, and now unwanted even by a cleaner's children. At this time he made the discovery that it was possible to feel, think or believe two contradictory things simultaneously. He felt proud and ashamed. He was glad to be out of the toy-box, and wished he was still in it. He worried about the future, and looked forward to better days.

This contrast of feelings was most noticeable when he considered the children. Here he was, a toy – a teddy, designed for children and put into the world for play. Yet he couldn't help thinking what barbarous creatures children were. To begin with, they were so messy; all sticky fingers and runny noses, and dribble in Baby Louise's case. The older ones had contests to see who could spit the furthest. On one occasion George and Denis had had a contest (private) to see who could wee the highest up a wall.

The bear was shocked by all this. It wasn't what his first romantic thoughts about children had led him to expect. More shocking still was the way the children behaved, the two girls especially. They seemed so often to make each other cry. Once he had seen Marjorie pull Kitty's hair for no reason. Another time he'd heard Kitty blame Marjorie for cutting a tablecloth (scissors again), when really it was Kitty who had done it. George, on the other hand, though naughty and dishonest, was also generous. The cat knew whose chair to sit by at meal times, if it wanted titbits. And when George got a lolly, everyone had a lick, even Louise.

The bear, observing these examples of generosity and spitefulness, was well able to tell the difference between them. He admired the one and was critical of the other. The only thing he didn't do was apply any of it to himself. His own spitefulness to the nervous bear, for instance, he simply failed to notice.

Well, the more the bear thought about children, the more he wondered why parents put up with them. If Marjorie could swop her toys with Shirley, which she often did, why couldn't Mrs Broom swop Marjorie?

Or send her back to the factory, even? That's what he'd do, if it was up to him.

THE WASH-HOUSE was cool and grey, and crowded. Before Mr Broom cleared it out it had been overflowing. It had a rough plank door with a latch, and gaps at top and bottom through which the wind blew. There was one small window with a broken pane (George!), and draughts came in through that. There was a sink below the window and a copper where the washing was boiled. There was a smell of smoke and laundry permanently in the air, a smell of oil from Mr Broom's bicycle and a smell of wood-shavings from his work bench. A rack of tools – mallets, chisels and such – was fixed to the wall above the bench. There was a smell of baby from Louise's pram, which during the drier months was usually kept there. There was a pong of boiled potato peelings and bran mash from the hens' daily feed prepared in the wash-house. There was the sharp odour of soot clinging to a set of chimney-sweeping brushes. These were stored by Mr Broom, but owned and used by the whole terrace. And, of course, there was a broom – the Brooms' broom (family joke).

On the shelf where the bear sat there was a watering can, a rusty tea caddy, a tin of Bluebell metal polish and the three alphabet blocks. The other unwanted toys were on the shelf below, together with a few late rejects, but minus the flat rabbit, which Kitty had recently crept in to rescue.

One morning – the day the holiday was to begin, as

it happened – Mr Broom arrived and rearranged the bear's shelf. He piled things up and placed a large square tin of nails next to the bear. It was a temporary measure. He meant to sort the shelves out properly after the holiday. (I may say Mrs Broom had just discovered these nails under her bed and was making a fuss.) When Mr Broom left, the bear looked at himself in the tin's shiny surface and was dismayed – no, horrified by what he saw. Was that scuffed-up and battered creature really him? He remembered the last occasion he'd seen himself – in the dressing-table mirror with Jemima – and how anguished he'd been then, when all he'd lost was a ribbon. A ribbon! Now look at him: his fur a mess, his paws faded, his legs squeezed out of shape, and his poor Louise-chewed ear.

At this point something surprising happened. Slowly, and hardly knowing that he did it, the bear raised a paw to touch his damaged ear. Yes, that's right – he moved. I know I said bears couldn't move, but all the same he did. The truth is, the subject of toys moving is more complicated than you were told. Most toys most of the time don't and can't move; but some toys some of the time can. It seems that if the urge is great or the emotion strong, a little movement can occur. For example, do you remember that baby bear in the factory startled by the cat? Well he moved, just a fraction.

There again, when you think about it, *tiny* movements of the head must be almost normal for a bear; otherwise he'd sit staring at one fixed spot for hours on end. But larger movements were rare, and, for that matter, unpredictable. What 'moved' one bear might well not move another. Our bear, whose passion was himself, was moved by the pity of his own appearance; the baby bear on the trolley by the shock of his first cat, and so on. Really large movements, though, such as running or jumping, never happened, which is probably just as well. The world, for children at least, would collapse into chaos if toys could simply run off when they felt like it.

As THE WEEK went by, life in the wash-house remained a dull and mournful business. It wasn't only the Broom family who had gone on holiday; almost the entire terrace had gone. This was the usual thing in that town in those days. Many of the factories shut down for the same week in August, and much of the population headed for the railway station. Here they clambered into steamy, smoky trains and rattled away to the seaside.

During that week the bear had no one for company and only a dripping tap and chirruping birds to break the silence. Each day out of the corner of his eye he watched the shifting shadows on the opposite wall. This wall was like a sundial to him; as the shadows moved, time moved too. It reminded him how Marjorie and Kitty had played at jumping on each other's shadows; and he wondered, as he'd wondered then, what a shadow was. Was it nothing? Was it real?

At night in the dark wash-house his sense of mystery, the strangeness of the world, was especially strong. Because of his position, he could not see the wheeling stars at the window. From time to time, however, he did observe a pair of tiny glittering eyes on the tiled floor. And that, for a bear still new to the world, was mystery enough.

THEN – hooray! – the holidaymakers returned. There was noise and bustle in the yard, laughter and shouting. The children brought their buckets of sandy shells and washed them in the wash-house, then left the shells and buckets *and* spades *and* fishing nets, and rushed off to play. Mrs Broom got a fire going under the boiler. By and by a pegged-out line of holiday laundry was flapping and smacking in the breeze. With other lines in the yard similarly full, it looked and sounded like a regatta.

Meanwhile the bear on his shelf was relieved and almost cheerful. Yes, children were dreadful at times, it was true; and play was a mixture of vandalism and madness – but what of it? Alone in a wash-house, that was worse. At least life went on around him now, even if he took little part in it. It was better than nothing. The bear, you will notice, was beginning to discover the value of companionship, and learning to be thankful for small mercies.

One of his favourite small mercies in the following days was Mrs Broom's singing. Mrs Broom was a frequent visitor to the wash-house. Mostly she engaged in the hard labour of washing clothes, sheets and suchlike. To keep her spirits up, she sang. She sang:

'When whip-poor-wills call
And ev'ning is nigh,
I hurry to my
Blue Heaven.'

The bear was captivated. He loved the sound of her voice, the lilt of the melody, and – although (or maybe because) he didn't fully understand them – the romance of the words:

'You'll see a smiling face,
A fireplace,
A cosy room;
A little nest
That's nestled where
The roses bloom . . .'

Mrs Broom didn't appear to know many songs.

48

Most, as far as the bear could tell, were about the weather. There was:

> 'You are my sunshine,
> My only sunshine . . .' (again).

and:

> 'Don't know why,
> There's no sun up in the sky,
> Stormy weather . . .'

Finally, best of all, there was this one:

> 'Look for the silver lining
> When e'er a cloud appears in the blue.
> Remember somewhere the sun is shining,
> And so the right thing to do
> Is make it shine for you . . .'

The bear had no idea what a silver lining was, but it didn't matter. The words gave him a feeling of hope, and he thought the tune was lovely. It also occurred to him at this time what a pity it was that parents didn't need toys. He'd rather play with Mrs Broom than Marjorie, any day.

Mr Broom came into the wash-house less frequently and mostly in the evenings after work. He pottered around sawing and planing lengths of wood or mixing the hens' feed. He whistled once in a while but didn't sing. George didn't sing either; he just sneaked in one Saturday morning, pushed some bits of firewood up his jumper, and sneaked out.

Marjorie and Kitty came more often, usually accompanied by various dripping toys, which they arranged on the draining-board. It was in this way that the bear met the panda again. The panda had recently formed one half of a swop between Kitty and Shirley. Now he lay on his back on the draining-board in a puddle, staring up at the bear's shelf.

'Is that you?' he said, observing the bear's feet. 'What's it like up there?'

'Boring,' said the bear.

'Never mind –' the panda coughed, a watery cough. 'You're well out of it, if you ask me. This is my third – (more spluttering) – bath in a week.'

But the bear wasn't well out of it, in his opinion. His cheerfulness, so recently acquired, had faded fast and despondency was taking its place. The worst part of being in the wash-house was hearing the sounds of children playing outside. At first he'd thought this was better than nothing, but now he knew it wasn't. And all the while there was the nagging shame of his rejection. When George had come in pilfering firewood, he'd had that ridiculous bear with him, a circumstance which our bear couldn't understand. He still considered himself superior, you see, inside if not out.

And so boredom descended on the little bear. Eventually not even Mrs Broom could cheer him up. He took to staring blankly at the opposite wall, ignoring the shadows and oblivious of the sounds outside. He thought: 'If only something would happen. Anything!' In this case small mercies were not enough; large mercies were needed. The bear was fed up with the wash-house and everything in it. What he could have done with was a silver lining, and the sooner the better.

Then, one day, the rag and bone man came.

[8]

The Rag and Bone Man

THE CHILDREN playing in the yard – it was the half-term holiday – knew the rag and bone man was coming long before they saw him. He had this penetrating cry, 'Raaag-aboah! Raaag-aboah!', which could be heard from streets away. The rag and bone man was a common sight in those days. He rode around the town with his horse and cart, collecting what he could: rags and bones, of course, but also pots and pans, jam jars, old iron baths, bedsteads, chairs – anything. He didn't pay for these things, but gave away balloons or paper windmills, or even, sometimes, day-old chicks. All this, as you might expect, was a ploy to get the children involved; and it worked.

On this occasion, for instance, no sooner was the rag and bone man heard than the yard became deserted. The children rushed indoors to pester their mothers. Shortly afterwards they were out again, clutching various bundles, or – in Marjorie and Kitty's case – rushing into the wash-house to see what could be found there. Marjorie and Kitty had a small sack and were working as a team to fill it. George was at his grandma's and missed the whole thing.

The girls entered the wash-house like locusts. Anything disposable went into the sack, plus one or two items that weren't disposable at all. The problem was, in those days poor families had little reason to give anything away. If it could be used as fuel, they burnt it. Old sheets were cut up for dusters, old coats and dresses for rag rugs, and so on.

The bear, meanwhile, was sunk in apathy on his shelf. He had hardly had a single thought in two days. He was so bored he couldn't even be bothered to think how bored he was. Then the girls came charging in and began grabbing things.

'This'll do!'

'And this!'

'Look what I've got!'

Away went the tin whistle and the incomplete jigsaws. Away went a ruined umbrella and a perfectly useful tin of Brasso. Away went a couple of things that Mr Broom had hoped might 'come in handy'. (Well, I suppose they had.) The bear was startled and confused. For a moment his hopes rose. He thought that Marjorie and Kitty must be playing a game. They might choose him. He would escape the wash-house yet. Then Kitty clambered up on to the draining-board to reach the higher shelves, grabbed the bear by his leg, and tossed him into the sack.

Oh, that poor bear! He couldn't understand what was happening, but something told him this was no game. It was dark and uncomfortable in the sack, and frightening. Worse still, as he was humped and dragged across the yard, he heard the rag and bone man's cry: 'Raaag-aboah! Raaag-aboah!' At once the bear's small fear expanded; it seemed to fill him *and* the sack. He didn't know about rag and bone men, not a thing; but somehow on this occasion experience was unnecessary.

The rag and bone man's name was Jack. He was a moderately ragged and bony man himself. He wore a jacket and a flat cap, and had a knotted scarf around his neck even in the heat of summer. His cart, pulled by a piebald pony, was loaded high with useful junk and festooned with paper windmills. As he turned the corner of their street, the swarm of children rushed to meet him; the cheeky ones calling his name, the brave ones patting his pony, the shy ones hanging back, and the timid ones back behind them. (Sometimes in those days an exasperated parent would tell a child, 'I'll give you to the rag and bone man, if you don't behave.' This explains the timidity.)

Well, the trading between the rag and bone man and the children took place. He examined their offerings, grumbled about the 'absolute rubbish' he was getting, piled stuff on his cart and distributed the windmills. At the same time he kept watch over his shoulder. There were children there capable of *un*loading his cart and offering things back to him. As Marjorie and Kitty stood in the queue, Mrs Broom examined their sack, just in case, and rescued the Brasso. (Of course, for a split-second as he glimpsed her face, the bear supposed she might be rescuing him.) Then, with a jolt, away went the cart and the rag and bone man, and away went the bear. He had no chance to say 'Goodbye', and no one, when you think about it, to say 'Goodbye' to, except the panda . . . possibly. Marjorie and Kitty waved, but not to him.

The cart went up and down a few more streets. The rag and bone man's cry still frightened the bear, but not as much as it had. A little light filtered through the rough weave of the sack. There was a smell of floor polish from a roll of lino laid across it. Far worse, there was a smell of raw meat from a bag of bones picked up earlier at the butcher's. There was a bundle of rabbit skins also.

From time to time the cart stopped and shouts of, 'Hallo, Jack!', 'Hallo, Monty!' filled the air. Monty was the pony. There were other sounds too. Sounds and smells, for now, were all the bear had. There was the roar of a bus and the honk of car horns, the rattle of the cart's iron-shod wheels and the clink of bottles and jars in its load. Finally, intriguing to the bear, there was another sound heard only when the cart stopped and the hubbub died away. It was a snorting, blowing sound, as though from some huge beast. But all it was was Monty, puffing with his heavy load and looking forward, doubtless, to a bag of feed.

Jack and his piled-high cart – he'd had a good day – reached Mrs Piggott's yard at half-past four. By now the bear had suffered in his sack for two hours. The panic about the rag and bone man was all but gone. Even so, a deeper fear remained. The trouble was, as always, not what had happened but what would happen next.

MRS PIGGOTT's yard appeared chaotic but was, in fact, quite orderly. It had a high wall and high iron gates through which the rag and bone men of the town drove their carts. They did the collecting and sold what they obtained to Mrs Piggott. She and her sons did the sorting, and sold it again: pots and pans to the scrap-metal merchant, bottles and jars to the glass-works, and so on.

Jack climbed down from his cart and stretched his legs. He gave Monty a nosebag full of oats. He went looking for Mrs Piggott. Meanwhile in his sack the bear's fear was expanding again. He could hear the crackle of a fire and smell burning. It reminded him of George. Actually there were two fires in the yard; they were kept going more or less all the year round. One was for burning the rubbish not even Mrs Piggott could sell; the other, a brazier for making tea and frying eggs, bacon and sausages. Mrs Piggott's sons – there were four of them – were a hungry lot. Breakfast was their favourite meal, which they were happy to eat at any hour of the day or night.

Soon, just as he had with the children, Jack began trading with Mrs Piggott. She examined his load,

peered into his sacks, grumbled about the absolute rubbish he was bringing her, and – eventually – offered him a price. Mrs Piggott, by the way, was a short wide woman in middle age. She wore a blue hat with artificial fruit on it as though she was off to a wedding. Around her considerable waist she had a potato sack which served as an apron. In her mouth she had a small unlit clay pipe.

Jack immediately protested at the price he was offered. 'Come on, Ma – you're robbin' me!' He began to demonstrate the superior quality of his goods. 'Look at this – solid brass! And these – worth quids!'

But Mrs Piggott was unimpressed. She raised her price, just a little – for friendship's sake, she said – and Jack reluctantly accepted it. The bear heard fragments of this bargaining with growing apprehension. Where was he? What was happening? Nor had he ceased to be concerned about the fire, which was still crackling.

Presently Mrs Piggott's sons came out of a hut seemingly too small to hold them, and the unloading of the cart and sorting of its contents began: metal to one pile, bones to another, and so on. The metal was destined for Pratt's (scrap-metal merchant); the bones for the glue factory; bottles and jars for the glassworks, and rags, clothes, bundles of old newspapers and cardboard boxes for the paper mill. Anything that didn't fit these categories was put on one side and puzzled over later. Oh, I nearly forgot – there was also a stack of worn tyres and pram and bicycle wheels in the yard. Mrs Piggott, for some reason, dealt with these herself. If people wanted tyres or wheels, they came to her.

So anyway, where does a bear fit into all this? Not metal or glass, obviously; and no use to the glue factory either, thank goodness. But a paper mill? Surely not. You can't turn a bear into *paper*. And yet . . .

Mrs Piggott's youngest son, Herbie – he was twelve – was rummaging in a sack. He tossed items skilfully to left and right, and by and by held up the bear.

'Hey, Ma – where's this go?'

Mrs Piggott glanced at the bear, and took the opportunity to educate her son. 'A teddy,' she said: 'fur fabric, that's cloth, outside; kapok, probably, or shavings inside. So where's it go? You tell me!'

Herbie frowned, and then, 'Paper!' he cried.

'Paper,' agreed his mother, and she took the bear from Herbie and tossed it away. (Actually, the truth is that Herbie might have kept the bear if his brothers hadn't been on hand to tease him.)

THE BEAR, dazed and bewildered, lay on a pile of old clothes and suchlike. He was upside-down which only added to his confusion. From his point of view, Mrs Piggott and her sons moved cleverly about the yard on their heads. Monty ate his oats with his feet in the air.

The fire blazed in the sky with a plume of smoke descending from it. But the bear gave little thought to any of this. He was trying vainly to make sense of what had happened. What was all that about kapok and paper, for instance? And what was he doing on this pile of rubbish? Had he been thrown away *again*, unwanted even by a rag and bone man? In the distance he heard the sizzling – and shortly after smelt the smell – of sausages frying in a pan. The sorting of Jack's cart was finished and Jack himself was on his way. The brothers were having a breakfast.

Gradually the sky grew darker: velvet blue, and purple, and black. A sprinkle of stars appeared, but no moon. The almost perpetual fires glowed faintly through the night. Meanwhile the desolated bear lay on his mound of rags and thought about his terrible life, until at last – relief! – he fell asleep.

9

How Paper Was Made

Paper can be made from various materials; these include wood, grass, straw and different sorts of cloth and rag; also waste paper and cardboard can be recycled. The process hasn't changed much since Victorian times. When the materials arrive at the paper mill, they are first of all sorted. In the case of cloth and rags, buttons and zips are removed and seams cut open. The rags are then chopped up and soaked in bleach and other chemicals to dissolve impurities. Later, depending on the kind of paper being made, the chopped-up and bleached rags are beaten for an hour or so, then forced between revolving knives to chop them more finely. The resulting pulp is poured out onto a moving belt of wire mesh. Gradually the water drains away, the pulp passes through various rollers, some of which are heated, and paper is formed.

THE BEAR was transported to the paper mill on the back of a lorry. He saw nothing of the journey since he was buried somewhere in the load. But on this occasion it didn't matter. He was not interested in the scenery, he was too busy thinking.

The bear had been thinking since six o'clock in the morning when the birds had woken him. It was eleven now. During this time he had reviewed his entire life so far and come to certain miserable conclusions. He was unwanted by the factory, unwanted by the children, unwanted even by the rag and bone man. His hopes had been raised and dashed a dozen times. 'A princess in a palace' – what chance was there of that? His mistake, he now believed, had been in trying to make sense of life, to understand it, when all the while there was nothing to understand. Well, not any more. If this was life, nuts to it (a phrase he'd learned in the wash-house from Mr Broom, when the woodworking wasn't working). Yes, from now on he would abandon hope and expect only the worst; and when the worst happened, he'd just put up with it.

THE LORRY was being driven by Albert, Mrs Piggott's eldest, accompanied by Herbie. It entered the mill gates, was weighed, and then unloaded and weighed again. There was a sort of monstrous weighing machine, called a weighbridge, set into the driveway especially for this purpose. By subtracting one weight from the other, the weight of the load could be calculated. Later on, subject to an inspector's report, Mrs Piggott would be paid accordingly.

The paper mill was a two-storey building: the offices and some storage space upstairs; the sorting and cleaning bays, bleaching tanks, pulpers and rollers downstairs. Well, the bear and his accompanying rags, dresses, odd socks and so on were piled into a number of large wheeled baskets under the inspector's watchful eye. (Cardboard and waste paper were also separated out at this stage.) The baskets were pushed into an enormous bay where they joined a line of similar baskets waiting to be dealt with.

In those days the preliminary work was done by hand. A number of women in green overalls sat side by side facing a conveyor belt. The contents of the baskets were spread out on the belt. As these passed slowly by in front of the women, buttons were cut off, pieces of elastic removed and unsuitable materials – woollens, for example – dropped into nearby bins. Further along the conveyor belt other women operated machines called 'dusters'. These sucked up unwanted dirt and fluff. As a matter of interest, in certain paper mills, though not this one, there was even a system for getting rid of undiscovered fragments of metal by cleaning the rags magnetically. Yes, and I bet they sold the metal to a scrap merchant, too. They didn't waste much in those days. On the other side of the town, for instance, at the glassworks, old bottles and jars went in, new bottles and jars came out. It was like a merry-go-

round. The glass had been going in and out of there
for years. If you think about it on a larger scale, this
circle of glass had lasted centuries. Bits of the most
ancient bottles – the Adam and Eve of bottles – are
probably still in circulation. What a thought!

Eventually it was the bear's turn to be dealt with.
His basket-load was spread out on the belt, and he
himself was carried slowly along towards the women.
Women not long ago had put him together; now, it
seemed, they were about to take him apart.

As luck would have it (luck!), the bear was sitting
up and facing the way he was going. He could see the
women in their green overalls, and the conveyor belt
disappearing into the distance. He could hear, above
the noise of the machinery, music playing. (The mill
often had the wireless on for the entertainment of its
workers. 'Workers' Playtime' was one of the programmes.) He could smell warm rubber (the conveyor
belt), the musty smell of old rags, and his own damp-
ness. He had been drenched in the dew that morning
back at Mrs Piggott's yard. But, though his senses
were in working order, he was taking little notice of
anything. He had begun to practise his new system of
ignoring the world and expecting the worst. Of course,
if he had known what the worst was . . .

On the other hand, attempting to blot out your
surroundings is easier said than done. The paper mill
was a huge and truly awesome place for a small bear, a
cavern of strangeness and noise. To pretend it wasn't
important, wasn't even *there*, was more than he could
manage. Besides, as the conveyor belt carried him

along, he could see the women in more detail . . . and what they were up to. Some of them had knives in their hands.

Yet still the bear sat up straight and tried to stop his brain from thinking. His brain, however, had a mind of its own. An image of Mrs Broom popped abruptly into it, for no apparent reason. She was standing at the sink, sleeves rolled up and pink-faced, scrubbing. The bear recalled the wash-house and wished he was back in it. Solitude, he could now appreciate, was not the worst thing in the world.

At this point, when all seemed lost, the bear suddenly toppled forward on to his nose, rolled sideways to the edge of the conveyor belt, and fell off. It is possible that, without realizing it, the bear had made an effort to sit up straight and had moved slightly, unbalancing himself. More likely, though, it was the uneven motion of the conveyor belt that brought about his fall. After all, it was not designed for carrying bears.

THE BEAR lay on the floor, the oily, rag-strewn floor, and took stock of his situation. He was off the conveyor belt, which appeared to be a good thing. *How* good he would probably never know. I mean, just think of it; if he'd stayed where he was, in a few hours a substantial part of him would have been turned into paper. And then – who knows? – made into a book, perhaps – about bears! (There's another circle for you.)

From where he lay, the bear could see the legs of the women and the legs of the chairs they were sitting on. But the women wouldn't pick him up; it wasn't their job. No, the sweeper would sweep him up, eventually, when he got round to it. After that, he – the bear, that is – would end up on the conveyor belt again. Oh dear, life was assuredly no picnic for this bear, was it? He was not out of the woods yet.

10

Mr Hardy

THE BEAR was picked up by Mr Hardy, having just been kicked by him. The kick was accidental, though. In a somewhat gloomy paper mill, a brown bear on a grey floor was not easy to spot.

Mr Hardy stooped and gathered up the bear. 'Hallo,' he said. 'What's all this? Trying to run off, are we?' Mr Hardy, I should say, was the general manager of the mill. It was his custom twice a day to visit each department and see how things were going.

The dazed bear looked up at Mr Hardy. He noticed his neat moustache and his sweet smell (Brylcreem). What he hadn't noticed, or hardly noticed, was the

66

kick. Given all that had happened to him lately, a kick was nothing. On the other hand – or foot – he would not have described it as an accident either. Everything seemed deliberate to him.

Mr Hardy looked down at the bear and smiled. What amused him was its expression. It looked so superior, and with so little reason. He walked on, intending to drop the bear into one of the baskets. Then, pausing, he put his foot up on a crate and gave his shoe a sudden shine *with the bear*. He smiled again – laughed, in fact – and continued on his way, taking the bear with him.

MR HARDY was a quirky man. He liked to surprise people and he liked to be different. On his desk there was a notice saying, 'THIS IS A NOTICE', his umbrella had a duck's head handle and his car was green, an unusual colour in those days. He enjoyed a joke and mostly saw the funny side of things. On April Fool's Day, though, he was a man to avoid.

Mr Hardy returned to his office and showed the bear to his secretary. 'Caught him trying to escape,' he said. 'Look at him; you'd think he owned the place.' He demonstrated the purpose to which he meant to put the bear. It was a good joke – a bear shoe-polisher – and not as unlikely as it seems. In those days people often used a small plush pillow to give their shoes a final shine. Mr Hardy had had one when he was a boy; the bear reminded him of it.

When he had finished shining his shoes, Mr Hardy strutted round the office to show them off. His secretary smiled and was impressed, or gave that impression. 'Very nice,' she said.

'Be better still when he dries out,' said Mr Hardy. 'He's a bit damp.'

At that moment there was a knock at the door and the stern-faced foreman of the Bleaching Shop came in. There was a problem that needed Mr Hardy's attention. Mr Hardy sighed, dropped the bear onto a chair and followed the foreman out. Alone in the office – the secretary had also left – the bear once more considered his plight. He was feeling as ashamed as he had ever felt. Here he was, saved from the conveyor belt only to end up as a duster. It was dreadful and, worse than that, preposterous. And he thought, 'Yes, that's it. Jesus wants me for a shoe brush.'

Well, this was the first joke the bear had ever made – the influence of Mr Hardy perhaps. In case you are unfamiliar with it, he was remembering the hymn 'Jesus Wants Me for a Sunbeam' that Marjorie and Kitty had sometimes sung when they came home from Sunday School. Not that he really saw it as a joke. It wasn't funny to him; and, of course, he had no idea who Jesus was.

Ten minutes later Mr Hardy returned. He made a couple of phone calls and filed the rough edge from a fingernail. He stepped up to a mirror hanging on the wall and straightened his tie. This was another aspect of Mr Hardy's character; he took a considerable interest in his appearance, from his shiny Brylcreemed head to his shiny brown-shoed feet. Rather like the bear, you could say he was in love with himself. The difference was, Mr Hardy was in love with – or had love for – other people too, especially Mrs Hardy and their little son; *his* name was Alfred.

At six o'clock a hooter sounded and the workers went home. Mr Hardy had a short meeting with the assistant manager, Mr Cork. At half-past six they left. By now the office cleaners were at work, emptying waste-paper bins – but saving the paper! – and polishing floors. The bear was perched high on a filing cabinet where Mr Hardy had left him. He watched the cleaner when she came in and thought at once of Mrs Broom and the bear factory. Perhaps *this* cleaner had a family. Maybe *she* needed a bear. Maybe . . . but, family or not, the cleaner never even looked in his direction. Soon the light was out, the door was shut and the bear was left alone.

The bear stared out into the soft black space in front of him, which at first was all he could see. As his eyes became accustomed to the dark, he began to distinguish certain features: the glimmer of light in the mirror; a pale glow at the window. There was a moon that night and presently the bear could see crisp shadows lying across the floor and furniture. There was a stack of boxes in one corner, a number of plants in pots around the room, a hat-stand and a gleaming desk. The cleaner, if she did nothing else, made sure of polishing that.

The bear was feeling better; not less ashamed but more resigned, and not so frightened. At the same time he was annoyed with himself. Despite his intentions, he had twice in the last few hours allowed his hopes to rise, only to have them dashed; recently with the cleaner, and before that with Mr Hardy. The bear's problem was that he couldn't help himself. His resolutions – to take no interest in the world and look only on the black side – were against his nature. Hope to him was like a worm to a fish, dangle it and he just had to bite (and never mind the hook). Also, the world was simply – complexly – such a startling place, so curious and new. He couldn't take his eyes (or ears or nose) off it. No, this bear was caught. He could no more ignore the world than . . . run away from it.

Take the telephone, for instance, which the bear could see on Mr Hardy's desk. What a strange thing that was. He had seen and heard Mr Hardy talking into that contraption and getting a reply, with *no one in the room*. There again, the bear thought, maybe that's how people make sense of the world. They phone somebody up and ask them.

The bear continued to observe the room . . . and think. There was a general smell of polish in the air: from the desk, and – regrettably – from the bear himself. Down the corridor, the cleaners' fading voices could be heard. They were leaving to go home. There was a distant hum of traffic, and a clock ticking. The bear was weary; he had been awake since six o'clock, remember. Slowly his thoughts unravelled into separate images: an upside-down horse; George crouched beside a fire; Jemima smirking. The bear stopped thinking altogether. He gave a sudden sigh and fell asleep.

That night the bear had his first dream, or the first one he remembered, anyway. In this dream he was running down the steps of a great palace, and a princess a lot like Kitty Broom was chasing him, and a queen even more like Mrs Piggott was chasing her. There were bonfires everywhere, and a crowd of people were watching from behind a barrier. They clapped and cheered and the children in the crowd waved paper windmills. The bear felt frustrated. He didn't want to be running away from the palace, he wanted to be back in it, playing with the princess. He also wanted a different princess. Then George came riding up on a horse.

THE FOLLOWING DAY the bear took up his duties as a shoe-polisher. Fortunately it was not as bad as he expected. Mr Hardy certainly used him to polish his shoes two or three times that day. But the next day he only used him once, and the day after that not at all. From then on the bear was used from time to time but mainly as a joke, a way of amusing visitors. Furthermore Mr Hardy had now acquired one of those plush pillows. He actually hadn't found it easy, shining his shoes with a bear.

The bear, meanwhile, was left with a polished patch on his front and a further dent to his self-esteem. ('Unwanted even as a duster.') He became, as the days passed, just another part of the clutter in Mr Hardy's office. (Mr Hardy, like Mr Broom, was better at acquiring things than getting rid of them.) During this period the bear overheard all sorts of conversations. He grew to understand the paper mill better, and its manager. He witnessed the number of times each day that Mr

Hardy looked at himself in the mirror: to comb his hair, trim his moustache, or simply, it seemed, to check if he was still there. It occurred to the bear that this use of a mirror was excessive. He also wished *he* could have a look.

On another occasion he heard Mr Hardy's secretary telling a woman that Mr Hardy was 'full of himself'. This puzzled the bear. 'Well,' he thought, 'I'm full of myself. What else could he be full of?' He thought some more, and half-guessed what the phrase might mean. He may even have noticed a similarity between himself and Mr Hardy. For the little bear was certainly changing; after all, he was six months old now. His sense of his own importance was not as strong as it had been − understandably, I suppose. His awareness of others, if not his consideration of them, was continuing to grow. It still didn't stop him from having unkind thoughts or being full of himself, but it was an improvement.

On the subject of other people, the bear learnt something from watching Mr Hardy. Mr Hardy always asked other people how they were and how their families were. Sometimes he opened the window and shouted down into the car park to ask them. Usually he offered his visitors a mint. The bear also observed the fond attention that Mr Hardy gave to the family photographs on his desk. Once, when no one was there to see except the bear, Mr Hardy actually kissed one of them. Every Friday after lunch Mr Hardy returned to his office with a bag of sweets and a children's comic, presents for his little boy. Often he spread the sweets out on his desk and counted them. Depending on how many there were, he allowed himself to eat one or two. It looked like liquorice was his favourite.

So during his days the bear had lessons in life from Mr Hardy, and during his nights he dreamed. To begin with the whole business of dreaming was a puzzle to him, a double puzzle really. Life was a puzzle, and here – inside it, so to speak – there was this other puzzle: dreaming. What's more he'd probably find another puzzle inside dreaming, if he kept looking.

Dreaming also exasperated him. A dream would be going well, delightful things would be happening, and suddenly it would veer off like a skidding car or, worse still, he would wake up. That was the trouble with dreams: you couldn't control them. Keeping a good dream going was a matter of luck. And, of course, not only that, there were bad dreams. One night he had a dream about Jemima and a pair of scissors, and *she* had the scissors. It frightened him so much that he struggled in the dream to wake himself up, and succeeded. Thereafter he sat for a whole hour in darkness – no moon – wishing he had someone to comfort him and fearful of what might be lurking in the room. At last a grey dawn lit up the window and he thought, not for the first time: 'What is a dream? What's real?' A brief memory of the shadows on the wash-house wall flickered across his mind . . . and he dozed off.

AFTER A COUPLE of weeks the bear lost his position on top of the filing cabinet. He was transferred to the window-sill, squeezed in between a small potted plant and a large glossy calendar. (The plant was a geranium, by the way; the calendar, the paper mill calendar from the previous year.) The bear sat with his back to the window. Though lower down, he still had a clear view of the room and what went on there.

One day, instead of sweets and a comic for his son, Mr Hardy came back to the office with a colourful cardboard box and a comic. Inside the box there was a bow, some arrows with suckers on them, and a circular target. Mr Hardy set up the target and tried shooting at it. Then he licked one of the arrows, stuck it to his forehead and staggered into his secretary's office. His secretary shrieked.

At which point the phone rang. Mr Hardy answered it. 'Hang on,' he said, 'I'll take a look.' He returned to his own office, went over to the window, opened it and shouted down into the car park. 'Harry – got Fred on the phone! He wants a word!' Then there was a knock at the door and the foreman of the Bleaching Shop came in. Something urgent had cropped up which needed Mr Hardy's attention. Mr Hardy, turning his back on the foreman, stuck the arrow to his forehead again, and made *him* shriek.

Meanwhile, with the outer door and window open, a gust of wind blew through the room. It blew some papers from Mr Hardy's desk and billowed out his secretary's skirt. It also caught the calendar on the window-sill, which responded at once like the sail of a yacht. In fact in sailor's language the calendar 'went about', which means it swiftly and powerfully swung sideways. Whereupon the bear, sitting next to it, received a sharp smack on the head, toppled backwards and fell out of the window – overboard.

11

The Dog

IT TOOK the bear one and a half seconds to fall to the ground. During this time he managed to think half a dozen different thoughts, which only shows how fast a brain can work, even a bear's brain. The rush of air reminded him of his trolley ride in the bear factory. A whiff of smoke on the breeze brought back the wash-house. There was also time to notice his dizziness as he tumbled head over heels, and be puzzled by Mr Hardy's last remark: 'He wants a word.' Yes, but what word, and what would he do with it? There was a brief remembrance, for no obvious reason, of his long-lost ribbon. And his final thought was: 'What next?' (The bear, you'll notice, wasn't frightened. Curiously, it seems, there was no time for that.)

As it turned out, the bear didn't hit the ground but bounced on the bonnet of a parked car. After that he hit the mudguard of another, and rolled out into the driveway where he ended up on his side. The second car had a woman in it who was just preparing to get out. The bear's sudden descent and noisy arrival startled her. She went to investigate. Unfortunately, in her haste the woman left the car door open long enough to allow a dog to escape. This dog was small, brown  and white, and incredibly energetic. He left the car like a cork from a bottle and began racing around.

'Billy – you bad boy!' shouted the woman. 'Come here!'

Billy at once trotted up, his tail wagging, an amiable – no, delirious expression on his face. As the woman stooped to grab him, he bolted again.

'Billy!'

While she was attempting to capture the dog, the woman looked around for whatever it was that had fallen from the sky. The dog likewise was exploring the car park, though in his case mainly with his nose and for different reasons. He paused here and there to mark his presence with a wee.

The bear heard the dog before he smelt him, and smelt him before he saw him. This was his first encounter with an adult dog; the puppy in the Brooms' yard hardly counted. All the same, his instincts warned him to expect trouble. The dog skidded to a halt in front of him, then pranced about, advancing and

77

retreating, inviting the bear to run off or play. Bravely the bear stared back at the dog even as its panting mouth and glistening teeth came nearer. Yes, he *was* brave; frightened but not panicking. Once more the dog darted at him. The woman appeared and shouted, 'Billy!' There was a shout, too, from Mr Hardy's window. The dog's jaws opened wide. The bear, in a futile gesture, slightly raised a paw to fend him off – and the dog grabbed him by it.

Thus began the worst four minutes of the bear's life (so far). The dog raced off with him, with the woman in pursuit. (She was more concerned to capture the dog, though, than rescue the bear.) His sharp teeth tore the bear's fabric in places and kapok came spilling out. Whenever the dog achieved a sufficient lead over the woman, who he assumed was playing with him, he stopped and waited. Sometimes he allowed her to get quite close before running off again. On one occasion she even managed to grab the bear by his leg, hoping to haul the dog in. But the tug-of-war was brief, the tears in the bear's fabric grew larger, and the dog won.

The dog also shook the bear, banging him left and right as a terrier (which he was) would shake a slipper or a rat. The bear, appalled and bewildered, hardly knew where he was. Then, suddenly, the worst horror of all: one of his eyes fell out! And the bear saw it – well, half-saw it, I suppose we should say. There was his eye – 'My eye!' – rolling away.

By this time Mr Hardy and his secretary were out in the car park helping the woman, who I can reveal now was Mrs Hardy.

'Billy!' they shouted.
'Bad boy – give it here!'
'Billy, you little blighter!'
'Drop it, I say!'
And, eventually, Billy did . . . drop it.

THE BEAR lay on the ground. Bits of his kapok were scattered about, one of his eyes was lost forever and his left arm hung emptily at his side. With his remaining eye he saw the dog, looking guilty now, being hustled back into the car. Presently the woman, Mrs Hardy, came over and picked him up. She began talking to Mr Hardy, who had joined her. The bear, as in an echoing tunnel, heard the words but made no sense of them. A dreadful numbness flooded through him . . . and he fainted away.

[12]

The Dolls' Hospital

WHEN THE BEAR came round, he was lying on a table with maybe a hundred eyes looking down on him. The eyes belonged to various dolls: pot dolls, rag dolls, wax dolls; large and small, dressed and undressed. Also present were a number of teddies, pandas, rabbits, what could have been an owl (it was hard to tell), and a zebra.

This gathering of dolls and soft toys was arranged on a series of shelves around the room. There were shelves on walls, a shelf above the door, and a narrow shelf, just big enough for miniature dolls, below the window. The window shelf was too low to allow a view of the table. Some of the other toys couldn't see it either, because they had their backs to it, or mob caps had fallen over their eyes. Finally, a few couldn't see it at that particular moment because two women were standing in the way. One of them was Mrs Hardy; the other was Mrs Finch, the owner and, you could say, doctor of this dolls' hospital, which was where the bear was.

Mrs Finch was examining the bear. 'My word, Anne, this is a poor little fellow.'

'That was my opinion,' said Mrs Hardy. She had her hat and coat off and was holding a cup of tea. 'Soon as I saw him, I thought of you.'

'Well, let's see . . .' Mrs Finch had a luggage label on which she was listing the repairs the bear would need. 'There's his arm, of course – have to be replaced. The joint's wrenched out – y'see?'

Mrs Hardy looked and nodded.

'And it was a dog, you say.' Mrs Finch frowned. 'Well, a dog never did all this. Look at these legs! Somebody's been wringing him out. Hmm . . . even his label's singed.'

The bear listened to Mrs Finch. He was still in a state of shock and only gradually realized she was referring to him. Immediately, however, he began to worry about the white coat she was wearing. It reminded him of the inspector at the bear factory and, worse still, the rejection bin. If they rejected him then, in all his glory, what chance was there now? But Mrs Finch had a soothing voice and a gentle manner. Despite his fears, the bear felt safe in her hands. The examination continued.

'What's this on his front?' said Mrs Finch. *'Polish?'*

'Polish,' said Mrs Hardy, somewhat shamefacedly. 'Yes, Norman's been using him . . . for a duster.'

'Has he? Hmm . . . he'll get a piece of my mind when I see him.' (At any other time the bear might well have thought: 'What piece?' But on this occasion the remark passed him by.)

Just then the doorbell rang. Mrs Finch left the room, followed shortly after by Mrs Hardy. Meanwhile the bear was experiencing a sudden rush of fear. It was a delayed reaction to Mrs Finch's reference to the dog. A vision of the dog's jaws loomed in his mind, and he shivered.

Around the room there was a flutter of tiny movements (heads mostly), and a hum of little voices.

'Hallo there!'

'Cheer up!'

'A dog had me once.'

'And me!'

The bear was lying on his back. He had a clear view of the ceiling and a confusing view of the shelves. He could see the zebra, for instance, which was a real puzzle to him. He struggled to speak. 'Where . . . where am I?'

And the little voices, some more sensible or well-informed than others, were quick to reply.

'On a table!'

'In a room!'

'Mrs Finch's!'

Then a gruff voice, rather louder than the others, said, 'It's all right. It's a 'ospital, mate.'

The bear moved his head a fraction and thought he could make out the speaker. It was a large, seemingly undamaged bear in a smart sailor suit. Confronted by so handsome a bear, our bear felt a quick pang of jealousy. This was followed, and for the first time in his life, by a quick pang of guilt for being jealous. Then he noticed the sailor bear had lost an eye. Whereupon the full horror of what the dog had done came rushing back. 'Oh, no!' he thought. '*I've* lost an eye!' And he would have cried, I'm sure, with the remaining one he had, if such a thing was possible.

At this point a dozen little voices whispered:

'Sh!'

'Sh!'

'She's coming!'

And Mrs Finch returned with Mrs Hardy.

Mrs Finch was a tall, grey-haired woman of about sixty. She had been running the dolls' hospital for thirty years. Her house was an amazing place, full from top to bottom with dolls and bears and dolls' houses and lead soldiers and rocking-horses and clockwork birds in cages, and much else besides. Children loved to visit it. Mrs Hardy when she was a girl had often come with her mother, who was a close friend of Mrs Finch's.

Mrs Finch reached under the table for a cardboard box, like a shoe-box with no lid. She sat the bear up in it, tied the luggage label to his leg and put the box on

a shelf. 'Now,' she said, 'you sit there a while. We'll soon have you as right as rain.' Then to Mrs Hardy she added, 'It'll be about a week. I'll give you a ring.'

THE BEAR sat in his box on the shelf. He could see dolls and bears – some of them in boxes, too – on the shelves facing him. He could also, now, see the table – the treatment table. It was covered with a white cloth. On a trolley next to it was an array of instruments: locking forceps, stringing hooks, pliers, scissors, needles, together with spools of thread and lengths of elastic. Around the room there were rolls of fur fabric and stockinette, bags of kapok and plaster of paris. In a box in one corner there were pieces of calico, velvet and felt. On the table itself there was a paintbox, a tray containing an assortment of glass eyes and the reclining figure of a small pot doll. The doll was beautifully dressed and apparently perfect, except that her head had come off. Mrs Finch had been in the process of putting it back when Mrs Hardy arrived.

Well, throughout the remainder of the day the bear watched Mrs Finch at work. He saw the pot doll with her head restored and heard her happy cry: 'Look at me!' (Mrs Finch was out of the room.) He saw a doll get new eyelashes and another have her mouth cleaned out and her lips repainted. (Her owner had been 'feeding' her and the food had set hard.) Finally, he watched as a rough, shapeless sort of creature that might have been an owl was given a new silk label. Actually it was its third label in four years, the previous ones all rubbed away by sleepy, hypnotized fingers.

84

The bear was soothed and fascinated by what he saw. Apart from her skill, Mrs Finch had a way with toys which astonished him. She handled them with great care, talked to them and took them seriously. The bear's hopes concerning his own injuries inevitably rose. 'I might even get a new ribbon,' he thought. Also he felt so much safer up there on the shelf, away from dogs.

MRS FINCH worked late. It was dark outside when she put out the light and left the room. The toys, alone now for the night, began at once to chatter among themselves. As you might expect, much of their conversation had to do with injuries.

'I've got a terrible big hole here.'

'My leg's just hanging on by a thread!'

'This baby sucked my shoe off – and ate it.'

There was a considerable exchange of sympathy and understanding between the toys. When a tiny infant doll who had lost all her hair began to sob quietly because she was afraid of the dark, *and* because she was bald, the others did all they could to comfort her.

The next main topic of conversation was 'owners'. Given that most of their injuries had been caused by owners, the toys were surprisingly loyal, not to say boastful.

'I belong to a little girl named Mary. She's only five and she can read.'

'My owner's name is Charles. His daddy is a banker.'

'My Jennifer's a big girl now. She has got a boy friend.'

Meanwhile the bear sat in silence, half-listening, half-occupied with his own thoughts. A faint light was getting into the room through a glass panel in the door. The bear was conscious of the lopsided quality of his eyesight and a curious 'pins and needles' feeling in his empty arm. Suddenly a ballerina doll sitting next to him and at a sufficient angle to see him said, 'You're a quiet one. What's your owner's name?'

Well, the sad, perplexed, ashamed and yet still proud bear glanced sideways at the doll, and didn't hesitate. 'George,' he said.

[13]

Mr Tump and Little Tump

URING THE NEXT two days the bear learnt the lesson, which most of us learn at some stage in our lives, that 'one lie leads to another'. The ballerina doll, as she waited to be repaired, became fascinated by the story of 'George', which the bear felt now obliged to tell her. George's remarkable family background and astounding achievements left the doll ever asking for more. The bear was almost as glad as she was when her repairs (loose legs) were completed and her owner came to take her away.

On the afternoon of the doll's departure, there was a great upheaval. Two men in white overalls and smelling strongly of paint arrived and began to fill up the room with chairs, a small bookcase, a dolls' pram full of dolls, a large, four-storey Victorian dolls' house, a piano stool, a rocking-horse and various other dolls and bears. (Most of these, I should say, were residents, not patients.) The miniature dolls on the window shelf went wild when they saw the house and declared, when the coast was clear, how much they longed to live in it. The incoming dolls and bears were accommodated on the shelves. Mrs Finch took charge of this. In our bear's case, she moved his box along and pushed two other bears in beside him. 'There we are – a couple of friends for you.'

When the work was completed and the men had left, the toys wondered aloud or asked each other what was going on. Whereupon the dolls in the pram explained.

'Mrs Finch has got the painters in.'

'The sitting-room needs brightening up, she says.'

'So she's moved us out.'

'Temporarily.'

The bear, for his part, looked at the bears who were his new neighbours. They were positioned on the shelf in such a way that he could see them and they could see him, but not each other. One of them was large. His fur was a light fawn colour; his eyes, greyish-brown. His head flopped forward slightly and he had big feet. His nose and snout were more pronounced than those of most bears. Some of the stitching of his nose was worn away and one of his felt paws was torn. He looked very old.

The other bear was smaller, half the size of the first against whom he was leaning. He had a cheeky expression and bright, almost orange eyes. He wore a short pullover with no sleeves, and one sock. (The other was on the floor nearby and would be returned to him presently.) His fur fabric was noticeably uneven; thick in places, bald in others. He looked old too, but not as old as his companion.

Both bears had a worn and faded, a cuddled look that reminded our bear of the bear in the factory, the one on display, the 'well-loved' bear. He remembered what he had thought at the time, about keeping clear of love if that was what it did to you. Now he wasn't so sure.

The little bear was the first to speak. 'Hallo! You're in a bad way. Who did all that?'

'A dog,' said the bear. Then, thinking about it, he added, 'And a man – and a boy – and two girls . . . and a baby.'

'Oh, they've been ganging up on you,' the little one said.

Suddenly the bear – our bear – felt the utter sadness of his life flooding over him. 'I had a lovely ribbon once,' he said, and sighed.

Now the big bear spoke. 'Cheer up, little chap. Life has its ups and downs.' His voice was deep – for a bear, that is – and his words came out in a measured way as though he had given particular thought to every one of them.

At this point Mrs Finch returned carrying a chair, which she stacked on top of another chair. She noticed the little bear's sock on the floor, picked it up and put it on him. Then she left.

'That's better,' said the little bear, who was now even more slumped up against the big one than before.

89

Our bear observed them both for a moment before asking shyly (he was mostly shy of the big bear), 'What have you got wrong with you?'

'Nothing,' said the little bear, 'except old age. We live here. I'm Little Tump and this is Mr Tump.'

'It used to be "Tomkins",' said the big bear. 'But it became altered over the years.'

'We are not related,' said Little Tump, 'just friends.' And he added, 'Anyway, what's your name?'

With some surprise, for he had really never thought about it before, the bear said, 'I haven't got one.'

'Oh!' said Little Tump. 'Well, what's your owner's name?'

The bear lowered his voice and this time spoke the truth. 'I haven't got an owner either.'

Whereupon a small high voice said, 'Yes, you have; his name's George. You told us all about him.' The speaker was an untidy-looking doll with a papier-mâché head, a squint, a knitted body and a partly unravelled foot. She was sitting at the back of the shelf eavesdropping now as she had done before.

The bear considered his options and decided to stick with the truth. 'No,' he said to the doll he couldn't see, 'it was just a story. I made it up.'

Once more Mrs Finch came back into the room. She took the sailor bear down from his shelf. His missing eye had been replaced. A plump little girl with plaits flying came charging in and joyfully received him. 'Look!' she cried to her mother, who was standing in the doorway, and she raised the bear aloft. Then boldly she clambered on to a chair and held the bear up to a mirror.

'Harriet!' exclaimed her mother, who was concerned about the chair.

But Harriet was not to be deterred. 'Sailor wants to see his eye!' she cried. And, of course, she was entirely right. Sailor did.

DURING THE REMAINDER of the day and into the evening the bear enjoyed the company of Mr Tump and Little Tump. They talked a great deal, all three of them. When Mrs Finch was working, though, or a visitor called, they kept quiet. But then, so it seemed to the bear, even the silence was companionable.

They talked about names, and Mr Tump explained that a name was simply what you were given: Mr Tump or Sailor or Piggy-Boo even, which apparently some poor doll on a lower shelf had been christened. There was not a lot you could do about it. 'And it's the same for children,' he went on. 'I knew a boy once, his name was Marmaduke. He didn't like it at all.'

They talked about their past lives. The bear gave a more or less true account of his time with Marjorie, Kitty and the others. (Whereupon the doll with the squint, still eavesdropping, declared, 'So there *was* a George!') Little Tump described an amazing toy shop and the Christmas-decorated window he had once sat in. Mr Tump recalled his early years with Mrs Finch's children, especially Miriam, who was his favourite, and he hers.

'Mr Tump knows everything!' said Little Tump in a sudden burst of enthusiasm. Although not so sudden, really, since he was enthusiastic most of the time. 'Guess how old he is?'

'I . . .' the bear hesitated.

'He's thirty-two!' cried Little Tump. 'Even I'm eight-
een. How old are you? Four, I'll bet.'

Well, our bear may have looked four or fourteen,
come to that, but the truth was – as I mentioned
earlier – he was just six months.

They talked about jokes, which Little Tump was
fond of telling, and the bear, as he got used to them,
fond of hearing. He especially liked the ones about
'The English bear, the Irish bear and the Scottish bear'.

In one of the longer silences the bear pondered this
new experience of 'friendship'. How comforting it was
to have someone he could talk to, who would share
his hopes and fears. Better still, how good it was to
forget himself for a while. Little Tump and Mr Tump
were a perfect combination. He could laugh with the

one and look up to the other. His affection for them grew with every hour. He had not had a superior thought all day.

WHEN NIGHT CAME and the room was dark, Mr Tump, at Little Tump's request, told a bedtime story. The bear had already noticed how the other toys nearby invariably fell quiet when Mr Tump was speaking. Now, with the added attraction of a story, the attentive silence spread still further. Only the miniature dolls with their miniature ears were outside the range.

The story was a long and splendid one, all about a girl named Miriam and her extraordinary adventures in 'The Land of Toys'. Little Tump said it was his favourite, though he also claimed it changed every time. Our bear was quite bowled over by the story. It was funny and sad, and utterly persuasive. He listened as though his life depended on it. He was desperate to know what the end would be, and hoping that the end would never come. Yet when it did he was entirely satisfied, as were the others.

And after that there was a collective sigh, murmurs of appreciation, and a swift and general sinking into sleep.

THE NEXT MORNING at nine o'clock Mrs Finch came in, took the bear from his shelf, placed him on the table and set to work. With a toothbrush and some white spirit she removed the polish from his front. With another toothbrush and warm soapy water she cleaned his fur. She removed his empty arm and extracted the damaged joint. She made a new arm and fixed it on. This, as you would expect, was by far the longest job. She had to sort through a pile of fur-fabric scraps to find something that matched, and a similar pile of velvet scraps for his paw. She had to measure – and draw – and cut out – and sew. (The sewing machine was in another room.) She had to fill the arm with kapok, carefully position the new disc joint and attach the arm to the body. After that the rest was relatively easy. Mrs Finch dealt with the loose thread on the other paw and tidied up the chewed ear. She selected an eye from the tray and stitched it into place. She also considered replacing the singed label, but decided not to. Finally she brushed the bear down with a stiff brush, studied him for a moment, said, 'There – right as rain!', and put him back on the shelf.

The bear experienced all this with mixed feelings. He knew, of course, what was happening, and wanted it to happen. But having an arm removed even when you know it won't hurt is still a disturbing business. And having an *eye* replaced . . . well.

All the same the bear came through his operation in good spirits. Towards the end he day-dreamed that some child might soon rush in and hold *him* up to a mirror. The prospects of an owner and a mirror were almost equally attractive. (His interest in his appearance was not over yet.)

Back on the shelf, his first words were: 'How do I

look?'

'Like a prince!' said Mr Tump.

'As good as new,' said Little Tump.

'Better than new,' the doll with the squint declared.

After that there was a general conversation about operations and repairs – Mrs Finch had gone to lunch – which led eventually to Frankenstein.

'What I think is, it's like Frankenstein,' said Little Tump.

'Who's Frankenstein?' said the bear.

'Er . . . I dunno.'

'He was a baron – in a story,' said Mr Tump.

'That's it,' said Little Tump. 'And he made a monster, out of bits and pieces.'

'What – a bear?' said the bear.

'No, a man!' And Little Tump laughed. 'Ha! Frankenstein's bear – that's a good 'un.'

During the afternoon the opportunities for further conversation were limited. A friend of Mrs Finch's arrived and sat drinking tea and eating biscuits with her while she worked. When evening came and conversation was resumed, the subject of new eyes, always a fascination for bears and dolls, was taken up. Little Tump wondered whether the bear's new eye *was* new or second-hand.

'Or third-hand!' he cried.

'Or thirty-third-hand!' added the doll with the squint.

'Just think of all the sights your new eye might have seen,' said Little Tump.

'Yes, and think of the tray, too,' said Mr Tump, gravely.

'That's true,' said Little Tump. 'That tray of eyes could well have seen a million things.'

'A trillion things!' said the doll.

For a moment there was silence as the mystery of the tray of eyes was contemplated.

Then Little Tump said, 'And there's your new arm, too . . .'

THE NEXT DAY in the middle of a conversation about all sorts of interesting things, like what was a hiccup, the bear was thrown into a sudden panic. The painters arrived once more and began *removing* chairs, the small bookcase, the dolls' house and so on. The miniature dolls grieved to see the house disappear (they had been making up a story about it), and the bear was heart-broken to think that his new friends were about to leave him. But then, as it happened, he beat them to it. For into the room as the painters left came Mrs Finch with Mrs Hardy. The bear was lifted down and admired. ('My word, I wouldn't recognize him.') Mrs Hardy did her best to pay Mrs Finch, but was firmly refused. The unhappy bear lay briefly on the table while the women went off to see how the sitting-room was looking. He called out in a quivering voice and with all his strength to his friends on the shelf.

'Goodbye, Mr Tump! Goodbye, Little Tump!'

And they called back, 'Goodbye, little chap!'

'Goodbye! Goodbye!'

Then Mrs Hardy came back into the room, picked up the bear and left.

[14]

All the Hardys

THE BEAR was on the move again. He was sitting in the passenger seat of Mrs Hardy's car, next to her handbag. It was a seat he had occupied before; but being unconscious at the time he had no memory of it. His brain now was a jumble of disconnected thoughts and feelings. To begin with he was frightened by the smell of dog, although the dog wasn't there and didn't, as it happened, belong to Mrs Hardy but to her mother. He could smell Mrs Hardy's perfume, which seemed to cheer him up. He was full of questions: who *was* Mrs Hardy? The only name he'd heard so far was 'Anne'. Where was she taking him? Why was she taking him? Who was 'Alfred'? Alfred had been mentioned a couple of times when they were leaving Mrs Finch's. There was some suggestion of the bear's being given to Alfred.

The bear was also curious about his surroundings. He couldn't see much because of his size. Even so, the glimpses he got – of traffic lights, trees, buses, horses, especially horses – fascinated him. There again, simply being in a car was a tremendous novelty. He felt better, too, because of his new arm and his eye. He hoped he might see himself soon in a mirror. Finally, however, hanging over everything else there was a cloud of sadness, a dominating sense of loss. The bear's new friends, his best friends, his only friends, were gone. It was worse than anything, he thought; worse than the wash-house or the rag and bone man's cart. He felt dejected and defeated. How unfair life was. It just picked you up and carried you off.

AND SO the dejected cheerful *fear*ful hopeful bear arrived at the Hardys' house. As you would expect, it was altogether larger than the Brooms' house. It was painted white, with a red tiled roof and a garage at the side. There was a gravel drive leading up to the front door.

Mrs Hardy carried the bear in and put him on a table in the hall while she removed her coat. The bear stared up at the ceiling. He felt nervous on his back, more vulnerable, like a tortoise. A parting remark of Mr Tump's came into his mind: 'Keep your chin up!' Guessing for once the larger meaning of this phrase, and despite the fact that he hardly had a chin, the bear resolved to try.

Mrs Hardy picked him up, held him behind her and tip-toed into the sitting-room. At once a familiar smell attracted the bear's notice, followed soon by a familiar sound.

'Guess what I've got?' cried Mrs Hardy.

And a man's voice (this was the familiar sound) said, 'A crate of beer! A wardrobe! A –'

'Not you, silly – Alfred,' said Mrs Hardy.

Whereupon, after a pause, a child's voice – Alfred's, of course – said calmly, 'hmm . . . a present, probably.'

Mrs Hardy, surprised by this response to her surprise, pressed on all the same. She made a noise like a fanfare, 'Da-daah!' and, with a conjuror's flourish, revealed the bear. Simultaneously, from the bear's point of view she revealed the boy and, for that matter, the man.

Mr Hardy was astonished to see the bear: 'My old duster – I'd never have known you.' The bear was fairly well amazed to see Mr Hardy. He had already smelt his Brylcreem and half-recognized the sound of his voice, but even so . . . Mr Hardy belonged in the paper mill. What was he doing here? The bear's main interest, however, was the boy. Alfred was a serious-looking boy. He wore glasses and was four and a half years old. He had his mother's curly hair and his father's round face. His character, though, as you will see, was entirely his own.

Well, Alfred received the bear with definite signs of pleasure. He thanked his mother and allowed her to kiss him. He carried the bear around for a while and manipulated his arms and legs. Later he tried to give him a ride in one of the carriages of his train-set, which was laid out on the floor, but the bear was too big. After that he left the bear in a sitting position next to the station and walked sedately from the room.

The bear . . . sat. He was bombarded again with sensations, from within and without. He was interested in the train-set and a curious-looking toy rabbit who at that moment appeared to be committing suicide by lying across the line. But this was just where Alfred had happened to leave him. Music was playing on the wireless, sunlight was streaming in at the window and a log was hissing and crackling on the fire. Mr and Mrs Hardy seemed to be having a cuddle. A wave of sadness overcame the bear as he remembered Mr Tump and Little Tump. This was followed by a wave of hope. After all, this looked like a good home for a bear. Alfred showed signs of being a civilized child. 'Life has its ups and downs,' Mr Tump had said. Well this was an 'up', wasn't it? Surely, yes, it had to be.

IN THE NEXT few days the bear became Alfred's second most popular toy. (The rabbit was the most popular.) Wherever Alfred went, he went. In this way the bear saw much of the house and garden, and made numerous trips in the car. When Alfred had his breakfast, the bear was there to see him eat it. When Alfred had his bath, the bear sat on a chair and guarded his pyjamas. When Alfred said his prayers, the bear knelt at the bed beside him. When Alfred slept, the bear was tucked in too, at the foot of the bed.

During this time the bear was able to observe the entire family, not to mention the rabbit, whose name was Roy. There were a number of surprises. Thus Mr Hardy might have been the boss of the paper mill, but he wasn't the boss here. No, the system was, as far as the bear could see: Mrs Hardy was the boss of Mr Hardy in a friendly sort of way, Alfred was the boss of Mrs Hardy in a calm sort of way, and Roy, on occasion, was the boss of Alfred.

The contrast between Mr Hardy and Alfred was also surprising. The one who was most excited by the train-set, or got scolded by Mrs Hardy for flying a balsa-wood glider in the house, was *Mr* Hardy. The calm one, who walked everywhere and had a row of pens and propelling pencils in the top pocket of his smart little blazer, was Alfred. This contrast was something of a puzzle to Alfred's parents. Mrs Hardy was a lively woman, Mr Hardy you know about, so how, they wondered, had they managed to produce Alfred?

'He's not like us at all,' Mr Hardy said on one occasion. 'Are you sure he's ours?' He picked Alfred up and stared at him. '*Are* you ours?'

'Yes,' said Alfred.

'Well,' said Mr Hardy to his wife, 'he reminds me of your Uncle Horace.'

'Me, too,' said Mrs Hardy.

'What a business,' said Mr Hardy and he laughed. 'You go to all that trouble to have a baby and you end up with your Uncle Horace.'

APART FROM the bear and Roy the rabbit, Alfred had few soft toys. There were a couple of plush penguins on a shelf in his toy-cupboard; there was an elderly camel that had been Mr Hardy's when he was a boy, and that was about it. The truth was, Alfred was more interested in cars, boats and planes.

Roy the rabbit, also known as Hopalong, was slim and rather stiff. His fabric, originally white, was now a dirty cream colour. He was dressed vaguely like a cowboy – named, in fact, after Roy Rogers and Hopalong Cassidy, favourite cowboy film stars of the period. He wore brown check trousers, a green waistcoat, a red and white striped shirt, and a red and white spotted neckerchief. He had the expression of an amiable dim-wit (which he more or less was): one eye noticeably higher than the other, and a mouth stitched into a perm-anent smile.

Inevitably, at first, the bear was jealous of Roy though he tried not to be. He couldn't understand what Alfred saw in him. From the foot of the bed each night he could hear Alfred telling Roy all sorts of things, and even seeking his advice. But in the bear's opinion Roy didn't know anything. When they had first met, for instance, and the bear was explaining where he had come from and all about the dolls' hospital, Roy listened for a while, said 'Oh dear!' a few times, and then asked right at the end, 'What's a hospital?'

All the same, Roy *was* amiable. He had the kind of nature which caused hostility to melt away. He wasn't funny like Little Tump or wise like Mr Tump, but at least there was no meanness in him. In time the bear came to appreciate Roy's good nature, while Roy – good-naturedly and from the very beginning – had nothing but admiration for the bear.

ONE PLEASURE which the bear and the rabbit shared was 'trips in the car'. The bear especially enjoyed the sensation of speed when Alfred or, occasionally, Mrs Hardy held him up to the window to look out. What Roy liked, when he got the chance, was joining in with the noise of the car – 'Brm, brm!' – something which he had picked up from Alfred.

Late one afternoon, returning from a drive in the country (to visit Uncle Horace, as it happened), Mr Hardy parked the car near the town centre. It was the end of November. The sky was overcast and darkening, almost brown in places. As the five of them (two toys, three people) got out of the car, it began to snow. The bear, of course, was delighted and entranced by his first snow, and even Alfred was excited. But the most excited was Mr Hardy. The snow was falling thickly. Before they had left the street in which they'd parked, there was a thin layer along the tops of the garden walls. Mr Hardy scooped some up and threw a snowball at Alfred, and got one back, and then another from Mrs Hardy. Roy was tucked into Alfred's coat; the bear in Mrs Hardy's bag. Alfred had instructed her to bring him along.

Now they were in the main street. They went into a butcher's and bought some sausages, and a newsagent's for Christmas cards. They passed a music shop where a man was playing a piano and singing in the window.

'You'll see a smiling face,
A fireplace,
A cosy room . . .'

came drifting out onto the cold air. The bear at once recalled the song and thought of Mrs Broom incongruously all hot and sweaty in the wash-house. Meanwhile the thickening carpet of snow had muffled the sounds of traffic and footsteps. The street lamps glowed against the ever darkening sky. The windows were ablaze with light.

Suddenly the bear felt himself plucked up out of Mrs Hardy's bag, and there before his eyes was an amazing toy-shop window. In the centre was a huge Meccano model of a big wheel, the sort you see at fairgrounds. It was powered by an electric motor and had various little toys, dolls and suchlike, sitting in its revolving seats enjoying the ride. Elsewhere there was a clockwork monkey playing a drum and a clockwork seal juggling a ball on its nose. There was a collection of skittles in the shape of guardsmen complete with busby hats, a toy fort besieged by soldiers, and a dolls' house all lit up with its own lights. There was a vast array of dolls and bears, roller skates and bagatelles, board games, books and jigsaws. For Alfred's especial delight there was no shortage of model cars, boats and planes. There was a toy submarine in a glass tank full of water and a toy gramophone with a stack of tiny records beside it that you could actually play.

Mr Hardy was holding the bear up to the window. Alfred was holding Roy. Mr and Mrs Hardy were talking to Alfred, finding out what he liked in the window and what toys he hoped Father Christmas might bring. The bear listened to some of this but most of the time his attention was otherwise engaged. The beauty and variety, above all the *newness* of the toys he could see, overwhelmed him. He remembered Little Tump's description of *his* Christmas window, but that was only words; this was the real thing. And then to top it all, to overwhelm his overwhelmedness, so to speak, there on a shelf at the side of the window the bear caught sight . . . of himself. Oh yes, it was him all right: same size, same fur, same velvet paws, same ribbon. Now already the bear had noticed, at certain angles, his pale reflection in the glass. So there they were; a brand-new version of his old self and a pale reflection of his present self: twins in a way, and yet . . .

The bear could have stayed and stared into that window for hours. He felt a bond of sympathy with all those brand-new (new-born!) toys, especially the bear, and had the urge to shout a greeting – or better still, a warning – through the thick glass. Soon, however, Alfred and his parents were ready to leave. In a little while they were back in the car and travelling cautiously along the snowy road. The last of the wintry light was fading from the sky. The brown fields and dark trees were disappearing under the snow. The head-lights of the car picked out the swirling flakes.

The bear sat on Mrs Hardy's lap. He was damp from the melting snow, but not as damp as Roy, who had been hit by another of Mr Hardy's snowballs. His thoughts – the bear's, that is – were in a turmoil again, like the swirling flakes outside. Seeing his reflection had cheered him up; he looked so much better. Seeing his old (new) self had saddened and perplexed him. Seeing a woman in a fur coat in the street had struck him as funny. Seeing the ghostly breath of everybody in the street – people, dogs, horses even – had scared him a little. He was intrigued by all this talk of 'Father Christmas', which was still going on. (Who was Father Christmas?) He was entertained by the smell (and the idea) of 'Turkish Delight', a box of which Mrs Hardy had stopped to buy on the way back to the car. But mainly it was the glowing image of the toy-shop window that continued to fill his mind. How new those 'new' toys were, he thought. How young! And he considered then the progress of his own life. So many things had happened in it – the factory, Mrs Broom, the rag and bone man's cart – and yet so many things could happen still. Time went running on ahead. Why, for all he knew, this was only the beginning.

[15]

The Education of a Bear

CHRISTMAS was coming. The sitting-room was hung with streamers and decorated with paper lanterns and silver cardboard bells. A real live Christmas tree in a tub of earth stood in one corner. It had chocolate decorations wrapped in gold paper, tiny presents, lights shaped like little candles and a fairy on top. The bear never actually saw the fairy – the positions he was placed in prevented this – but he saw everything else, and loved it. He loved the way the Christmas cards kept accumulating on the mantelpiece, and the smells coming from the kitchen. There was an increasing sense of bustle and excitement in the house. The doorbell rang, the phone rang, a pile of presents grew beneath the tree, and Mrs Hardy had a hard time stopping Mr Hardy from opening some of them. Even Alfred abandoned his usual solemn stroll and took to running everywhere.

But the main attraction, no, fascination for the bear was Father Christmas. Who *was* Father Christmas? His picture was on many of the cards and also the cover of Alfred's comic. His name was on everyone's lips. But who was he? And where was he? And how did he get down the chimney if the fire was burning? And how did he get back up? And where was the North Pole? And what was a reindeer?

These and similar questions were discussed by the toys whenever the opportunity arose, which was mostly at night when Alfred was asleep. The old camel, whose place was on the mantelpiece, said he knew who Father Christmas was but he wasn't telling. The penguins said it didn't matter because they knew anyway. They were out of the toy-cupboard at this time and passengers in a wooden lorry parked near the end of the bed.

'There is no Father Christmas,' they said.

'It's Mr Hardy.'

(I should add that these penguins had been bought as a pair and tended to speak as a pair.)

'It's the same in the shops.'

'All men – dressed up.'

Roy on the other hand said he believed in Father Christmas very much – and Alfred would hang a stocking up for him like he did last year – and he would get a present – which was a chocolate snowman last year – which was lovely – only Alfred ate it.

The bear was understandably confused. He didn't know what to believe. Later on, on Christmas Eve, he tried to stay awake and see for himself who Father Christmas was. This was the penguins' idea. But of course none of them managed it, while the camel didn't even try. The next thing the bear knew, the bedroom light was on and Alfred was sitting up in bed with his Christmas stocking and his Christmas pillowcase. Roy was admiring *his* stocking. There was wrapping paper strewn across the bed and floor. Temporarily the bear was buried by it. New toys and games, a pair of mittens, a *Rainbow* annual, a couple of balloons, some sweets, an apple and an orange, were rapidly emerging. By and by the bear identified a number of the toys as ones he'd seen in the toy-shop window. But whether Mr and Mrs Hardy or Father Christmas had brought them from the shop, he was unable to decide. No, the mystery of Father Christmas, for the bear at least, was a mystery still.

PREDICTABLY the new toys occupied most of Alfred's attention in the next few days. The older toys had every reason to feel put out, especially the bear. He was no longer the second most popular, or the third, or even the tenth. This decline in his popularity had actually begun before Christmas. Often he had been left in the bedroom for hours on end while Alfred played downstairs. Trips in the car had become infrequent and eventually ceased altogether.

Why this should have happened is not easy to explain. The combination of life's experiences and Mrs Finch's clever fingers had certainly improved the bear's character and appearance. His new eye was fractionally better placed than the one he had lost, and it made all the difference. In fact, really the squint-eyed doll (do you remember her?) was right. In this respect the bear *was* better than new. His mouth still had that slight superior curl to it, but overall his expression was less off-putting than it had been. At the same time he was now noticeably more aware of others, more considerate of them and less full of himself.

Take what happened with Teddy Fudge, for instance. Teddy Fudge was one of the new toys, a home-made knitted bear. He wore a pair of white knitted shorts with a matching jumper. Not long after his arrival he acquired a tiny necklace of bakelite beads (actually, a bracelet), which Alfred had found in a cracker. Teddy Fudge was not well made. His filling — a kind of sponge rubber — was clearly visible in places and a tuft of wool stuck up comically from one of his ears. As for his expression (and therefore, character), he was even dimmer than Roy. All the same, Alfred took a liking to him. Teddy Fudge was promoted to number one toy; well, number one soft toy; the absolute number one was a submarine in a glass tank. Roy accepted this situation with his usual good grace. More surprisingly the bear — our bear — accepted it also. He had been disappointed for some time about not getting a name. In the early days Alfred had considered naming him, and Mr and Mrs Hardy had offered helpful suggestions, although Mr Hardy's were not always that helpful. But nothing came of it. Now, lo and behold, along comes this ordinary little bear and he gets a name straight away. Alfred thought of it himself; he had developed a fondness for fudge and, besides, it matched the bear's colour.

Yet despite his disappointment and demotion our bear behaved well towards his new companion. He defended him when the penguins made fun of his bakelite necklace. He told him some of Little Tump's jokes to cheer him up when he said he was homesick. Apparently Teddy Fudge was one of a large family of knitted bears; the work of Alfred's Auntie May. They had observed each other being knitted during most of the past year, felt part of the same ball of wool, so to speak, and were distressed at being separated. The truth is, when he looked at Teddy Fudge, the bear was reminded of the nervous bear that George had taken a liking to. He recalled with shame his unkind words and jealous thoughts. He only wished there was a way he could go back and make amends.

THE DAYS and weeks went by and the bear got used to being neglected. After all, he had had plenty of practice. From time to time Mrs Hardy brought him downstairs and sat him on the dresser in the kitchen. Mrs Hardy, I believe, still had a lingering sense of guilt about what the dog had done. She was a soft-hearted woman altogether. In the evenings the bear received

occasional attention from Mr Hardy. (I think he felt guilty too.) Mr Hardy tucked Alfred up each night and read him a bedtime story. Sometimes he sat the bear or Roy on his knee and pretended to let them see the pictures. Well, he was pretending; the bear and Roy, of course, were actually seeing them. But these were isolated instances. The sad fact was that for much of the time, as the bear himself realized, he was once again . . . unwanted.

Nevertheless things could have been worse. The bear felt *some* shame and disappointment, naturally, but not as much as on previous occasions. For one thing, being neglected by Alfred was no great loss. Alfred's ideas of play were dominated by vehicles and clockwork, all rather boring from a bear's point of view. Furthermore there were consolations. For example, in the kitchen with Mrs Hardy the bear was able to listen to the wireless. He especially liked the music – dance bands and songs – and one or two of the comedy programmes. He did his best to remember some of the jokes and passed them on to Teddy Fudge and Roy. But his favourite programmes at that time were 'In Town Tonight', in which famous visitors to London were interviewed, and the six o'clock news. The bear's education and knowledge of the world were greatly extended by these programmes. He learnt who (and what) the Prime Minister was, the name of the capital city of France and the length of Europe's longest river. He heard about King George VI and Adolf Hitler,

Stanley Matthews and Amy Johnson (he was a foot-baller; she, an aviator). One programme which the bear would certainly have liked was 'Children's Hour'; but Mrs Hardy usually listened to this in the sitting-room with Alfred, and somehow the bear never got to hear it.

Another source of education for the bear was Mr Hardy's bedtime stories. They were not as good as Mr Tump's stories, but they were intriguing all the same. I mean, could you really make a man out of gingerbread or a coach out of a pumpkin? (What was a pumpkin, anyway?) Then there was 'Goldilocks and the Three Bears'. Here were these bears – who according to the pictures looked much like our bear – and they were living by themselves and capable, it seemed, of going for walks and eating porridge. It was fantastic.

The remaining strand in the bear's education was provided by Roy and Teddy Fudge, and to a lesser extent the old camel and the penguins. Each night they discussed all manner of things: Alfred's character, Alfred's birthday, which was approaching, the Grand National, what a zip was, what a burp was. A recent visit from Alfred's cousin, a girl addicted to burping, had prompted this.

They tackled larger subjects too. In particular they talked a lot about God. Hearing Alfred say his prayers each night had obviously pushed this topic to the front of their minds. Who was God? – that was what the bear wanted to know. Had he got anything to do with Father Christmas, for instance? And why did Alfred say his daddy was a 'heathen' because he didn't go to church on Sundays? Mr Hardy's answer to that was, 'It takes all sorts.' But what did *that* mean?

Roy said he believed in God, Jesus, Father Christmas, Easter Bunnies and anything else. The penguins on the other hand claimed to know for certain that there wasn't a God. The world was made by 'evolution', according to them. The camel said he knew who God was but he wasn't telling.

One night Teddy Fudge came out with a hymn he'd recently remembered, which Alfred's auntie used to sing:

> 'All things bright and beautiful,
> All creatures great and small,
> All things wise and wonderful,
> The Lord God made them all.'

'There you are,' said Roy. '"The Lord God made them all" – that proves it.'

'No it doesn't,' said the penguins.

'Ask yourself – who made Him?'

Whereupon, of course, the conversation became really complicated: Who made God? Who made the God who made God? Who made the God who made the God who . . . and so on. The bear, for his part, was reminded of a set of Russian dolls which Mr Hardy had given Mrs Hardy for Christmas: a doll within a doll within a doll. It was all too puzzling for words. It made his brain ache just thinking about it.

At that moment Mrs Hardy came in on her way to bed to give Alfred a kiss, which she usually did. The conversation ceased and did not resume after she'd left.

Presently Mr Hardy came in and sat looking at the sleeping Alfred for a while. Then he left, and the toys dozed and dreamed until another day.

THE WEEKS and months went by. Alfred's birthday duly arrived, and later on so did the bear's, though he never knew it. There was a memorable day in early summer when Mr Hardy went wild in the garden

with a bubble-blower. For half an hour the garden *and* the house were invaded by lovely translucent rainbow-coloured *fragile* things. The bear watched with delight as they floated and popped around him. On another occasion, also in the garden, the bear received an unpleasant surprise. A familiar penetrating cry sounded in his ears: 'Raaag-aboah! Raaag-aboah!' It was the rag and bone man, Jack, again. But Jack was (luckily) out of luck this time, as far as the Hardys' household was concerned.

In June of that year the Hardys had planned to take

a holiday at the seaside. The bear explained to Teddy Fudge what a holiday was, what a seaside was and, finally, what a sea was. Teddy Fudge, by the way, was no longer the number one toy. Roy had long since regained this position.

Well, the holiday was planned but it never took place. You could say 'clouds' gathered to prevent it. During this period Mr and Mrs Hardy took to frowning a good deal. They listened intently to the six o'clock news, read bits of the newspaper out to each other over breakfast and made anxious phone calls to their relatives and friends. It was a bad time for the Hardys, a bad time for everyone, in fact, and threatening to get worse. The air and airwaves, the papers and people's minds were full, you see, and frantic . . . with rumours of war.

[16]

A Bear Alone

How a war is made: to make a war you need two sides, just as you do for a fight in the playground. In this particular war, which was about to begin, the Germans were on one side, and the British and the French were on the other. (By the end, though, more than sixty countries were involved.) The other things you need for a war are weapons: bows and arrows in the old days; tanks, battleships and bombs in the 1940s, and so on. Usually, once a war had started, most people expected it to end much earlier than it did. For example, this one was expected to last a year or two, and it lasted six.

In the first year of the war Mr Hardy gave up his

job at the paper mill and went away to become a soldier. Actually, he'd hoped to become a pilot in the R.A.F., but his eyesight wasn't good enough. Jack, the rag and bone man, became a soldier as well; so did Albert, Mrs Piggott's eldest. While Mr Hardy was away, Mrs Hardy and Alfred, together with the bear, Roy and the others, gradually became accustomed to the peculiarities of wartime life. There was the 'black-out', for instance. This meant having black curtains up at the windows so that no light was visible to enemy aircraft. It also meant that whenever Alfred's bedside lamp was out his room was pitch dark, a circumstance which Teddy Fudge in particular found scary.

Then there were the gas-masks, which everybody – man, woman and child – was required to have and carry with them. Gas-masks were needed in case of an attack with poison gas. Our bear thought Alfred looked funny when he tried his on, and Alfred thought Roy looked funny when Mrs Hardy tried it on him. Later on, however, Roy said it wasn't funny at all. He didn't like the cloudy perspex mask, the horrid smell of rubber and the feeling of being trapped.

Another thing which upset Roy at that time was rabbit pie. As a result of the war meat became scarce. One day Mrs Hardy served rabbit pie for dinner. Alfred indignantly refused to eat it and put his hands over Roy's ears to stop him even hearing about it. Roy heard, though, all the same.

The aspect of war which the bear disliked most was the air-raid siren. This was a loud wailing noise which went off as a warning whenever enemy bombers were approaching. It was such a dreadful and menacing sound that it caused the fur on the back of the bear's neck to stand on end, although to begin with there were no bombers and the siren sounded just for practice.

Well, the first time it did go off, Mrs Hardy grabbed Alfred (and Alfred grabbed Roy) and down they went into the cellar until a second siren (the 'all clear') sounded. Meanwhile the horrified little bear sat on the landing, where he had been left, with no one to comfort him at all.

Not long after this Mr Hardy came home on leave, looking smart in his uniform and with a liquorice pipe in his mouth. He had liquorice pipes for Alfred and Mrs Hardy too. While he was home, and with a neighbour to help him, Mr Hardy dug a huge hole in the garden and assembled an air-raid shelter in it. Air-raid shelters were supplied by the government. They were made from curved sheets of galvanized iron bolted together to form a sort of tunnel. This was buried to a depth of about four feet, with earth from the hole piled on top. From then on, whenever the sirens sounded, Mrs Hardy and Alfred went down into the shelter.

IN THE SECOND year of the war, by which time the bombs *had* begun to fall, it was Alfred's turn to go away. Mrs Hardy arranged for him to stay with his auntie in the country where she hoped he would be safer. Alfred took with him a small suitcase mostly full of clockwork cars. He jammed Teddy Fudge into his raincoat pocket and carried Roy. The bear, along with the camel, the penguins and other less precious possessions, he left behind.

Mrs Hardy, as you can imagine, was terribly upset by Alfred's departure. She cried a great deal and sought to distract herself with extravagant and exhausting bursts of spring cleaning. The bear too was miserable. Though he made every effort to be brave, the now familiar sensations of shame, rejection and loss swept over him. He missed Alfred, but even more he missed his friends Roy and Teddy Fudge. He worried about the bombs – he could hear and *feel* the occasional distant thud of them – and hoped his friends were safe. Well Teddy Fudge, as it happened, was safer than safe, or so *he* thought. You see, the auntie that Alfred had gone to was the very one – Auntie May – who had made Teddy Fudge, and all the other Teddy Fudges, in the first place. He had returned, as you might say, to the bosom, or the ball of wool, of his family.

So Teddy Fudge had his family, Roy had Teddy

Fudge, Alfred had them all – and the bear had nobody. He must have felt that life was shrinking around him. And yet . . . even now consolations could be found. In the absence of her husband and son, Mrs Hardy set up shrines of photographs and mementoes around the house. The old camel and the penguins found a home on the mantelpiece in her bedroom, and the bear lived almost permanently in the kitchen. He sat on the table next to a potted plant that grew steadily but never seemed to flower.

Mrs Hardy had taken a job to help with the war effort; she drove a bus. But when she was home she spent much of her time in the kitchen. Each morning she waited anxiously for the postman to arrive. Letters from Alfred, helped by his auntie, were frequent; letters from Mr Hardy, less so. (Mr Hardy, now Corporal Hardy, was far away on the other side of the world in a place called Burma.) When letters did arrive Mrs Hardy had the habit of reading them aloud, to herself and also, it seemed to him, to the bear.

Another pleasure which the bear and Mrs Hardy shared, which they had shared before, was the wireless. It was during this period that the bear heard what turned out to be his favourite programme ever: 'The Brains Trust'. This was a programme, broadcast weekly, in which a panel of clever people answered questions sent in by listeners. The bear, although he often failed to understand the questions, let alone the answers, soon grew to love this programme and luckily Mrs Hardy was attached to it too. There was a professor whose voice he especially liked; it reminded him of Little Tump (though his brains reminded him of Mr Tump). What's more, the programme covered such a variety of subjects: weather forecasting – the habits of the common snail – the meaning of 'History'. Indeed, as the months went by, and although he didn't know it at the time, the bear was becoming wiser. Then, still in the second year of the war, Mrs Hardy went away.

Mrs Hardy went away because the bombing was getting worse – a recent bomb had narrowly missed the bus depot – and because she couldn't stand the separation from Alfred any longer. She cancelled the papers and the milk, turned off the water, gas and electricity, moved various potted plants out into the garden to fend for themselves, arranged for the post to be sent on, packed a suitcase, put on her hat and coat, and left. On her way out she paused for a final look around the kitchen. She removed a snapshot of her husband from its frame and put it in her bag. She looked at the bear, and the bear, who well knew what was going on, looked at her. As you might guess, the thought in his mind was, 'Take me as well! Oh, please – take me!' But Mrs Hardy left without him.

And now the bear was quite alone. As the days and then the weeks went by, the kitchen clock ticked loudly in the empty room, and ceased to tick. A spider spun a web across one corner of the window, the biggest web the bear had ever seen, and then abandoned it. Dust descended from the air and settled on the cooker and the kettle, the table and the chairs, the sink, the taps, the curtains . . . and the bear.

To begin with the bear endeavoured to be brave.
Life had its ups and downs, he knew this now and was
prepared to wait for better times. 'I am not finished
yet,' he told himself. And he was philosophical too. He
recalled a true story that Mr Tump had told to illustrate
the perplexing business of 'luck'. It concerned a terrible
disease called scarlet fever, which a boy had had. In
order to destroy the germs, everything was burned:
blankets, pillows, books, toys – everything. Mr Tump,
however, escaped this fate because he had been left in
the summer-house. (He was there for two whole years.)
He had fallen under a bench and been accidentally
kicked still further out of sight. That was 'luck', said
Mr Tump and thirty years later here he was to tell the
tale. Just a little fall and a little kick that would have
seemed like bad luck at the time . . . that's all it
took.

The bear found consolation, too, in the ever changing scene at the window. The unpruned rose bush
'rose' and spread across the lower panes; budded,

bloomed and faded. A pigeon regularly perched and strutted on the sill. Bees blundered against the glass. Above all, though (above all!), there was the sky itself: an endless mystifying scroll of clouds and stars that moved across his vision.

In addition to all this, if hardly consoling, there was the war to be seen. On one occasion for an entire week a barrage balloon, sent up to hamper the bombers, tugged and heaved on its cables like a mighty silver elephant, and then was gone. Planes also came and went. At night searchlights frequently split up the sky, or swooped from end to end of it. Flares, dropped by the bombers to illuminate their targets, flooded the town with an awful light. Often on the horizon or nearer still the fierce red glow of burning buildings could be seen.

Gradually as the months went by the evidence of war grew less: fewer sirens sounded, fewer bombs fell, fewer searchlights searched the sky. And the leaves on the rose bush yellowed and browned, and began to blow away. And the bees buzzed off.

Sadly, by now the bear was sinking into apathy. He'd done his best to keep his spirits up, but it was no use. In earlier times he might have managed better, for in those 'superior' days he'd needed no one but himself. Now his life made little sense when others weren't around to share it. By slow degrees he had become a sociable bear.

Down went the bear, and down and down into what, I suppose, was a kind of hibernation. For a while faint wisps of memory still drifted in his mind: Alfred

with a toy tin hat and wooden rifle; George and his
suspiciously bulging jumper; Little Tump, smiling. But
eventually even these faded. Dust gathered on the
bear's eyes and dimmed his vision. Finally, like the
kitchen clock he just stopped ticking altogether and sat
there.

And then, one night, a bomb fell on the house and
blew it all to smithereens.

[17]

Is This the End?

THE BEAR was horribly frightened. He was upside-down in a small black cave of splintered wood and broken brick that might collapse at any moment. The blast had blown him clean across the room, even as the room itself was disappearing. A rush of scalding air had singed his back and pretty well charred his label. He was deaf in one ear and one of his arms was pinned beneath a broken teapot. An acrid smell of soot and smoke stung in his nose.

After a while the bear heard muffled shouts somewhere above his head (well feet, really), and two or three blasts on a whistle. Still in a state of shock, he began to say his prayers: 'Our Father we chart in heaven' – he had picked this up from Alfred – 'Hallowed be Thy name.' At that moment he remembered the penguins – 'There is no God' – but continued praying none the less. A fire-engine bell clanged faintly in the distance. The bear began to make some sense of where he was and what had happened. Then, for the second time in his life, he fainted.

THE NEXT MORNING when the sun came up the devastation in the street was plain to see. The Hardys' house was a monumental pile of rubble. Neighbouring houses had had their windows blown in and, in many cases, lost their chimneys. Fences were flattened, hedges scorched and a tree lurched crazily across the road. A lamp-post was bent over like a drinking straw. In the middle of somebody's garden was a ridiculously twisted bicycle and half a car. Everywhere was littered with bricks and brick dust, tiles and shattered glass and plaster. By the way, the bomb responsible for all this was called – would you believe it? – a 'nuisance' bomb. At this stage in the war regular large-scale bombing had ceased. Instead, from time to time, a solitary plane flew over . . . to make a nuisance of itself.

Meanwhile below ground the bear was conscious, though he would rather not have been. A sense of absolute despair enveloped him. He was unwanted – isolated – lost – abandoned – trapped – and buried alive. Actually, because of the particular way the house had collapsed, he wasn't all that buried (but that was *no* consolation). A little daylight, even, filtered into his cave and the sounds of workmen beginning to clear up impinged upon his good ear.

Slowly as the hours went by the bear's jumbled thoughts became more orderly. He identified the scrape of a shovel and a shouted name: 'Henry!' He worked out that he was upside-down. He remembered sitting in a sack on the rag and bone man's cart, and being buried under piles of rags in Mrs Piggott's lorry. (Why, that was years ago.) The smell of soot and smoke was fading. A current of fresher air blew faintly through his fur. Lodged in the wall of the cave was a fragment of a picture frame, which the bear recognized, and the handle of a saucepan. Nearby, sharing the cave with him, he spotted a piece of wax fruit – a pear – that was, amazingly, undamaged. He recalled his previous amazement with the very idea of wax fruit: was it made or grown? Who needed it? What was it for?

Gradually the sky grew dark outside, though some light still found its way into the cave: there was a half-moon shining. The bear – calmer now, but no more cheerful – attended to the multitude of sounds around him in the ruined house: sifting plaster, creaking wood, shuffling bricks and tiles. In a curious way, the house – though flat – had hardly finished falling yet.

The bear was weary. He tried to sleep, but failed; tried to hope, but couldn't. Eventually he even tried to move . . . nothing happened. Vibrating through the rubble, he heard – and felt – the far-off sounds of traffic. Water was dripping somewhere near his good ear; above him in the 'normal' world it had begun to rain. Then, later on that night, the first of the rats arrived.

The bear heard them before he saw them – a rustling sound, and squeaking; after which a pair of scrabbling paws with a twitching nose between came burrowing into the cave almost on a level with the bear's own nose. To begin with there were two of them: an adult and a baby. Of course, this place – a dungeon for a bear – was a perfect home for rats, and heaven probably for a baby rat: one house brought down to a convenient rat-sized pile.

The rats didn't waste much time. They rapidly explored this little space they'd found and took possession of it. They even stood up on their hind legs to examine the roof. The bear was both afraid and, curiously, unafraid. His instincts told him to beware of rats, but these particular ones were upside-down as he saw them, and consequently comical. What's more the young one smelt strongly of strawberry jam. Its snout and paws were sticky with it, like a naughty child – Kitty, for instance – up to mischief in the pantry. Nevertheless, as the bear was shortly to discover, a rat's a rat for all that. Its eyes are beady, its teeth are sharp, it has an appetite for almost anything and no conscience whatsoever.

The first occupant of the cave to suffer was the wax pear. The baby rat skidded with teeth and claws across its polished surface before gnawing a chunk out of it. Soon, preposterously soon, a third of the pear had disappeared. (How did it go with strawberry jam, I wonder?) Meanwhile the adult rat had begun experimentally to *eat the bear*. In quick succession it sampled fabric, velvet and black thread. It seemed unable to decide which it preferred. For a moment the bear was petrified. Just think, the horror of it — to have your own *mouth* eaten. What made it worse, this rat was so close he couldn't actually see it, couldn't focus on it. But after that the bear hit back. With a spasm of panic and defiance he kicked his legs – and growled.

It wasn't much of a kick really, or much of a growl, but it impressed the rats. The movement of the bear's left leg dislodged a lump of plaster from the roof of the cave, which walloped the adult on its snout and caught the baby a glancing blow. The growl echoed menacingly in the enclosed space. With a fair display of panic of their own, the rats turned tail and ran – or rather, scuttled – colliding as they did so with a third rat, which was just nosing its way in. Well, this one got the message too, and quickly vanished.

SOME TIME LATER, when the fog of plaster dust (and fear) had faded, the bear took stock of his situation. He felt decidedly better: he'd seen the rats off *and* produced a growl. The damage he'd suffered was not great, and was, in any case, largely invisible to himself. (Kapok had spilt from his rat-chewed paw and part of his mouth was missing.) At that moment an upside-down spider appeared and halted in front of him. The bear admired it. What delicate legs it had; how jauntily it moved. The spider departed. Next the bear's attention was caught by a strip of wallpaper attached, in fact, to the lump of fallen plaster. This paper had the prettiest pattern, all flowers and leaves. The bear had seen it before – in the hallway – but never appreciated it until

now. By this time it was getting lighter in the cave.
Dawn had arrived, and far away – down a tunnel, so it
seemed – birds were singing. A little surge of cheerfulness ran through the bear. And the thought in his
mind was: 'I am not finished even yet.'

THE BEAR slept, though it was early morning now,
and dreamt for the first time in his life a realistic
dream, as opposed to a fantastic one. He dreamt of
Alfred having treacle in his tea because of the sugar
rationing; Mr Hardy home on leave admiring himself
in the sitting-room mirror while Mrs Hardy was out
of the room; Mrs Broom still hard at work at the
wash-house sink; Roy in his gas-mask.

The bear awoke. The light was stronger. Boys'
voices overhead were shouting: 'Hey – wait for me!'
'Stop shovin'!' Suddenly a foot (plus boot) came crash-
ing through the roof of the cave, missing the bear –
and the pear – by inches. A boy's voice swore. The
foot disappeared. The bear was dazzled by a flood of
brilliant light. And then a hand appeared, with dirty
fingernails, the bear had time to notice. It grasped his
leg, tugged for a while to release him from the broken
teapot, then raised him up into the open air . . . and free-
dom.

[18]

My Blue Heaven

THERE WERE three boys altogether: Trevor Sadler, Brian Sorrell and a small red-haired boy who was only ever referred to as Hipkiss. They had been roaming the bomb-site, which the Hardys' house now was, in search of military souvenirs, in particular fragments of the bomb itself. It was against the law, of course; for one thing they were trespassers and for another taking things like the bear, or a toasting fork, which Brian had picked up, was, well – stealing. However, rats are rats, boys are boys, and finders keepers.

Trevor was the one who'd found the bear. He was a tall boy for his age – he was eleven – with a mostly serious expression.

'Hey, Trev, what y'got there?'

'Trev's got a teddy!'

'Shut up,' said Trevor. He held the bear in one hand and poked the loose kapok back into its damaged paw with the other. He brushed the bear's face and front with the sleeve of his coat.

'Trev's got a teddy!'

'Shut up.'

Meanwhile, as the boy studied the bear, the bear studied the boy – and the other boys – and the bomb-site – and the *beautiful blue sky*. There was joy in his heart to be out of that terrible hole in the ground, and hopeful thoughts in his mind. This boy, for instance, he looked reasonable enough; a bit scruffy maybe, a bit old perhaps, but still . . .

Just then there was a warning cry from Brian: 'Look out!' Immediately the bear found himself confined again, this time buttoned up in Trevor's coat. Through a gap in the buttons – the coat was a tight fit – he glimpsed what was happening.

A policeman on his bicycle had stopped in the street. 'What's all this?'

The 'innocent' boys approached him.

'Morning, Mr Bird!'

'Just looking for our ball.'

The policeman took a handkerchief from his pocket and blew his nose. 'Don't give me that. I'll tell your dad, young Hipkiss, when I see him.' He blew his nose again. 'Now then – hoppit!'

The boys plus bear plus toasting fork departed. They collected Brian's bicycle from the kerb and walked sedately away. The policeman watched them go. The street was more or less clear of debris now and the damaged lamp-post had been removed. As the boys turned the corner out of sight, they became themselves again: talkative, animated, urgent. Brian rode his bicycle, standing up on the pedals, Trevor sat on the saddle and Hipkiss ran alongside. The bear felt a cold breeze on his face, or rather that part of his face that was peeping out from Trevor's coat. He was uncomfortable; it was a bumpy ride. All he could see was the back of Brian's jumper.

The boys rode and ran from one street to another, passed the cemetery and in and out of the park. They argued constantly about where they should go, which route they should follow, whether Hipkiss should get a turn on the bike, whether a so-called bullet that Brian had found was really a bullet (it wasn't), and so on. At one point – in the park – they stopped and argued with two other boys. Brian swopped his toasting fork with one of them for some cigarette cards. Trevor was teased again about the bear. Later, when Hipkiss had got his breath back, he related the entire story of a film he claimed to have seen at the Imperial. It was a horror film, the most horrible horror film ever, according to him. The others scoffed. Hipkiss was too little and too young to get in to such a film, in their opinion. They refused to believe him. The bear believed him, though, or rather he believed the story. It scared him somewhat, even in broad daylight in the open spaces of the park. He remembered what Little Tump had said about Frankenstein and bits of bodies, and he shivered. There again he might have shivered anyway, for the sky had clouded over and it was getting colder.

Out in the street, while Trevor pushed the bicycle, Hipkiss and Brian played marbles in the gutter and argued about the weather: 'whether' it was going to rain (Brian) or snow (Hipkiss). Twenty minutes later a heavy miserable sleet descended from the sky, and both claimed victory.

The boys went home; Hipkiss one way, Trevor and Brian the other.

Hipkiss ran backwards up the street, shouting as he went, 'I'll call for you!' And then, 'Hey – what y'gonna do with that bear?'

Trevor shrugged. 'Nothing,' he said.

Hipkiss fell over, jumped up, kept running – 'I'll call for you!' – and was gone.

Brian had his scarf up over his face like a bandit. At Trevor's house he pulled the scarf aside and said, 'What *are* you going to do with it?' But the sleet was falling faster now and already Trevor was halfway down the path. 'I'll call for you!' said Brian, and he rode away.

135

TREVOR SADLER lived in a council house with his mother, his grandmother, and his younger sister, Sophie. His father was a petty officer in the Merchant Navy. Trevor hurried down the side of the house and opened the back door. He peeped in. He could hear his mum and grandma talking in the kitchen. Noiselessly he closed the door, crept down the hall and tiptoed up the stairs. In the safety of his room, Trevor took off his coat and tossed the bear on to the bed. From the gap under his wardrobe he removed a biscuit tin. This tin contained his secret collection of cartridge cases, the fin of a bomb, a piece of parachute, a number of army and navy cap badges, and a German propaganda leaflet. Trevor spread his collection out on the floor, admired it for a while and put it away.

The bear was face down on the eiderdown, and apprehensive. 'What *is* he going to do with me?' he thought. He heard the worrying clink and scrape of metal, and was reminded of Marjorie and her scissors. It occurred to him then what a truly unknown quantity strangers were. (It's surprising he hadn't noticed this before.) He thought of George. He thought of Frankenstein.

Trevor picked him up, examined him for a moment, dropped him back on the bed – face up this time – and left the room. The bear stared at the ceiling. There was a funny smell in the air – the glue from a balsa-wood model Trevor was making. Sleet was rattling against the window. Up through the floor the faint sounds of music from a wireless or gramophone could just be heard. The bear's deaf ear, by the way, was getting back to normal.

Trevor returned. He had with him a needle and thread, some brown paper, a pair of scissors (scissors!) and a ball of string. He sat on the bed. With much squinting and licking of fingers he threaded the needle. He took the bear on to his lap and proceeded to stitch up the hole in his paw. It was not the first sewing Trevor had ever done, but it nearly was. He put a couple of stitches in another, smaller hole in his left leg. He spat on his handkerchief and wiped the bear's still somewhat dusty eyes. He trimmed, like trimming a moustache, a couple of loose threads from his mouth. He snipped off the charred label. After that he spread the brown paper out on the bed . . . and wrapped the bear up in it. Finally he tied his parcel securely with string and carried it from the room.

DOWN IN THE KITCHEN Trevor's mum was toasting a teacake by the fire, his grandma was darning a sock and Sophie was sitting at the table painting a picture. Actually it was a 'magic' painting book; one of those books where you applied water with a brush, and the colours (of a sort) magically appeared (or were supposed to).

In came Trevor, looking serious, with his parcel hidden behind him.

Mrs Sadler glanced up from her toasting. 'Hallo, love – where've you been?'

'Playing,' said Trevor.

'Where?'

'Here and there,' Trevor shrugged. 'The park.'

He made his way to the table. Sophie had her head down and her tongue out. She was concentrating on her picture.

'What're you hiding?' said his grandma.

'Something,' said Trevor. He crouched down to the level of the table in order to see Sophie's face. 'For Sophie.'

Sophie looked up and Trevor put the parcel on the table, well clear of the jam jar full of water. Inside the parcel, the bear's thoughts were racing. Maybe he should have guessed he was a present – he'd seen enough parcels at the Hardys' house after all – but he didn't. Being wrapped up was scary, like being an 'Egyptian's mummy'. He had only a vague idea what an 'Egyptian's mummy' was – he'd heard about it on 'The Brains Trust' – but that was the thought in his mind. Furthermore the brown paper crackled whenever the parcel was handled, preventing the bear from hearing what was said. He couldn't tell what was happening or, worse still, what would happen next. Suddenly, the walls of his paper prison were torn apart and the bear could see . . . a smiling face (well, two really) . . . a fireplace (as he was lifted up) . . . a cosy room.

As soon as the bear saw Sophie, he *understood* what was happening. Sophie, I should say, was four and a half years old, the same age as Alfred, although come to think of it Alfred was seven now – Kitty was eleven – Marjorie was thirteen! Sophie held the bear and looked at him. Mrs Sadler left her toasting and came to look at him too.

'Oh, Trevor – what d'you want to give her that for? Scruffy object.' And then, suspiciously, 'Where'd you get it?'

Trevor had his story all prepared. 'I swopped for him – with Kenny Cutler.'

'What did you swop?'

Trevor mumbled something, at which point his grandma came to the rescue. She had joined the others at the table. 'Well, it's got a nice expression, I'll say that for it.'

'Nice expression?' said Mrs Sadler. 'It's filthy.'

All this time, of course, the bear was in suspense. It didn't matter to him what the others had to say, he hardly heard them. What mattered was what *she* had to say: Sophie.

Sophie continued to look closely at the bear, while Trevor looked closely at Sophie, and Mrs Sadler looked closely at him. Sophie's gaze was solemn. Moments later she put the bear back on the table and walked away. The poor bear by now was frantic. Something told him this was his last (best) chance. 'Oh, no,' he thought, 'not again. Please let her like me. Please!'

Mrs Sadler, meanwhile, was questioning Trevor in more detail about his swopping activities, the condition of his hands – 'like toads' backs!' – and whether he had been messing about on those bomb-sites again. Sophie returned (from a visit to her grandma's sewing-box). The bear looked up. Actually, from the position he was in, he had little choice. He saw a smile on Sophie's face, and a *red ribbon* in her hand. She picked him up and tied the ribbon round his neck. The bear was overjoyed. (Move? He could have turned a cart-wheel!) Sophie held him out to show her mother and to thank her brother. Finally she clutched him closely in her arms and spoke the words the bear had waited all his life to hear: 'I want him.'

SO THERE WE ARE: one bear, one home, one happy ending. Thanks to Trevor and his scissors, and the rats – thanks to the bomb – thanks to Mr Hardy and Mrs Hardy, and Mrs Hardy's mother's dog – thanks to Mrs Finch and Mr Tump and Little Tump – thanks to Jack, the rag and bone man, and Marjorie and Kitty and George – and Mrs Broom – and 'The Brains Trust' – thanks also to the paper mill calendar (do you re-member that?), and the fall from the conveyer belt – thanks to the new arm and the new eye, and the rest of the bear too, come to that, for he was a factor in his own life, that's for sure – thanks above all, I suppose, to the women in the bear factory, the finishers, the misplaced stitches and crooked eyes – yes, thanks to all these things (and a few others!) the bear was who he was and where he was.

Later that day the sleet stopped, the sun came out and Brian and Hipkiss called for Trevor. Sophie and her still-reluctant mother – 'You never know where it's been!' – gave the bear a wash and brush-up. With a nail brush and soapy water they removed the dirt, soot and plaster from his fur and sat him in front of the fire to dry. In the evening, while Sophie had her bath – in a tin bath also in front of the fire – her grandma tidied up Trevor's sewing. She made a better bow of the

bear's ribbon. As she sat in the easy chair admiring Sophie, she gave him a cuddle.

Bedtime came. Sophie carried the bear up to her room. She introduced him to a knitted rabbit with button eyes. She tried a blue crocheted coat on him, which had been hers when she was a baby. Her mother and grandma tucked her in and switched the light off, though the landing light was on and the bedroom door ajar. Sophie snuggled down with the bear in her arms and the rabbit on her pillow. She began to talk: 'It's Sunday School tomorrow ... My daddy is a sailor.'

After a while Trevor put his head round the door. He came over to the bed and crouched beside it. Sophie held the bear up for them to see each other. Trevor shook him by the paw.

'What will you call him?' he whispered.

'I will call him ... Teddy,' Sophie said.

Trevor left, and slowly Sophie drifted off to sleep. Her arm remained around the bear and her warm

breath touched his fur. With only the slightest movement of his paw, the bear returned her cuddle. He
would not sleep for ages yet. His heart and mind were
just too full. He was, of course, the happiest of toys: an
altogether *wanted* bear.